DOUGLAS  re and in

Cont

**The item should be returned or renewed
by the last date stamped below.**

Dylid dychwelyd neu adnewyddu'r eitem erbyn
y dyddiad olaf sydd wedi'i stampio isod

Newport
CITY COUNCIL
CYNGOR DINAS
Casnewydd

To renew visit / Adnewyddwch ar
www.newport.gov.uk/libraries

The book is well written, well plotted and the main characters engage our sympathies from the outset. The murder and detection elements are woven well into the historical aspects of the book. The descriptions of how witches were identified and dealt with are both fascinating and horrifying.
FICTIONFAN on *Testament of a Witch*

Edinburgh is one of the book's main characters, and Douglas Watt has caught the rhythms of the great city – its pulsating politics, its strict religious codes tempered by bawdiness, and its grasping love of commerce and money.
CRIMESQUAD on *Pilgrim of Slaughter*

Watt skilfully reconstructs the political events of the period and weaves a convincing mystery around them.
LOTHIAN LIFE on *Pilgrim of Slaughter*

The identity of the murderer will keep you guessing until the very end and the idea a murderer is on the loose during the turmoil of the revolution keeps the pages turning. A must-read if either murder mysteries or history are your thing.
NICKY COOPER BROWN on *Pilgrim of Slaughter*

A Killing in Van
Diemen's Land

DOUGLAS WATT

Luath Press Limited

EDINBURGH

www.luath.co.uk

First published 2021

ISBN: 978-1-913025-45-8

The paper used in this book is recyclable. It is made from low
chlorine pulps produced in a low energy, low emission manner
from renewable forests.

Printed and bound by iPrint Global, Ely

Typeset in 10.5 point Sabon by Lapiz

To Julie

*All manner of sin and blasphemy shall be forgiven
unto men: but the blasphemy against the
Holy Ghost shall not be forgiven.*
Matthew 12:31

List of Main Characters

JOHN MacKENZIE – advocate

DAVIE SCOUGALL – writer

CHRISSIE SCOUGALL – wife of Davie Scougall

JOHN DALRYMPLE, MASTER OF STAIR – Lord Advocate

JACOB KERR – merchant

MARGARET KERR – wife of Jacob Kerr

MARY KERR – daughter of Jacob Kerr

JANE MONTGOMERY – servant of Jacob Kerr

AGNES CAIRNS – servant of Jacob Kerr

THOMAS CAIRNS – son of Agnes Cairns

ALEXANDER FRASER – student

Scotland, 1690

CORRUPTION FIRST STIRRED in my soul long ago and has grown like a tumour within me ever since. One moment I am happy in the worship of the Lord, the next fallen into deepest despair. I become a creature tossed and turned by every wind of temptation, blown here and there like a boat upon the ocean of the world.

When I blow out my candle in my chamber at night, I tremble in the darkness, my mind filling with dreadful visions which will not leave me all night long. I get no rest during the hours of blackness. I am beholden to my thoughts and ruled by them, sometimes until the light of dawn peeps through the awning and birds begin to sing.

During the night, all my sins are presented to me. I know them like the lines on my hands. My sins are these: my want of the love of Christ, my pride, both natural and spiritual, my hypocrisy and my backsliding. In the wake of these lesser transgressions comes much worse – the perverse notion of disbelief infects my thoughts. God help me through this vale of tears!

When I am afflicted by sin, whether in my chamber at night, or on the causeway during the day, or even in the house, I hear words spoken inside my head. They are so clear that I know not if they are from my own being or from some other creature biding within me. Such loathsome words that I dare not commit them to paper. I believe there is no other creature in the whole world so bound to sinning than me.

There is no temptation out of Hell that I am not bewitched by. When Satan sees all his temptations are yielded to, he presents the final sin to me. It is the worst sin of all. It is the mother of all sins. It is the sin of atheism.

As my corruption grows day after day, night after night, I am tempted more and more to call out aloud and blaspheme to the wide world, proclaiming my sinning nature to all, even during the hour of holy prayer, or in the Kirk as the minister preaches, or even at the table during Holy Communion, when I should be covenanted with the Lord. I have an aching desire to shout out such things as: *The words written in the Bible are fancy. They are not the words of God, but the contrivance of men. The ministers are not servants of God but seducers of the people.* These words are on the tip of my tongue. At such times, I fear I am not known by Him. I am cast out of His house. You are nothing, I say to myself. You come from nothing. You pass to nothing. You deserve nothing. How can you be promised everlasting life when you are a vile sinning creature who doubts the existence of God?

I cannot be rid of such thoughts. The temptation to think them is always with me, especially at night when it rises to fever pitch. But more and more, such thoughts spring up, unbidden, during the day. I desire more and more to proclaim my life is a sham, holy form without, while at my core, I am festered by sin.

I know who is responsible for my torture. I know who speaks within my head. I see him in my mind's eye. Sometimes he is just a presence, a sense of foreboding. Other times, he is a corporeal creature who watches me in the fields beyond the city walls or in the woods. Satan walks among us, the minister tells us. We must be on our guard for him. We must watch out for the Tempter. Satan throws stones of sin at us. Some are pebbles which I swat away like flies, others are rocks which pierce my skin and send me reeling.

As I grow in my sinning, there comes into my mind one sin more agreeable to my nature than all the rest. It squeezes the others out of my thoughts, like the cuckoo displaces its rivals from the nest. I call it my predominant. It is like a beautiful jewel absorbing the eye and which the heart desires. I encourage it. I keep it in my heart hidden from all. It returns each night. I fight it with all my strength but cannot be rid of it. It enflames my mind with visions so depraved that, when I recall them in the light of day, I shudder to the pith of my bones.

When sin has me in its grasp, tight as a vice, I grow weary of everything and fall into lassitude. I feel a deadness of spirit. I am overcome with a desire to sleep, even during secret prayer, when I am usually full of vigour and joyous in the Lord. I am like a stone at the bottom of the ocean, crushed by the vast weight of water above. I am nothing but a hypocrite. I am the vilest creature ever born in the world. God has surely cast me from his holy vessel and abandoned me to drown in an ocean of sin. Then, the temptation to misbelieve sweeps through me. It is irresistible unto my mind. *There is nothing, there is no God*, I say to myself again and again. *There is no Saviour. There is no Christ. There is no Redemption.* I forget the mighty works of the Lord. The wise words of the ministers are sand in the wind. I see only the corruptions in my nature which render me vile. I dare not look at my face in the glass lest I see the Devil's mark on my countenance. I repeat the words again and again, countless times in the chamber of my mind. *There is no Christ. There is no Redemption. There is no God.*

CHAPTER I

A Meeting with the Lord Advocate

'CONGRATULATIONS ON BECOMING a grandfather', said Dalrymple, looking up with a hint of a smile on his pale face. He sat behind a huge desk, on which two candles flickered, the only source of light in the dark, windowless chamber. Dressed entirely in black, his body seemed to meld with the surrounding darkness, accentuating his ghostly features and the whiteness of his wig.

Rosehaugh was Lord Advocate the last time MacKenzie had sat in this room. Rosehaugh was now gone – swept out by the revolution two years before, just as MacKenzie was swept out of the Court of Session. The world was indeed turned upside down, although some things remained the same. The Lord Advocate's office was the same dismal, stuffy chamber. The same grim paintings covered the walls, depicting previous Advocates, just perceptible in the shadows. MacKenzie doubted Rosehaugh's portrait hung among them yet. The revolution was still raw and its final outcome was perhaps uncertain.

'I'm twice blessed, my Lord', MacKenzie replied. 'My daughter is returned to me after her…', he hesitated for a moment, searching for the right words to describe Elizabeth's elopement with Ruairidh MacKenzie, '…adventure in the Highlands. And I have a grandson at the Hawthorns.'

'I'm pleased to hear it.' Dalrymple's expression reverted to its usual stoniness. 'Have you heard anything of your chief?' he asked casually, rotating the quill in his right hand.

MacKenzie had to be careful with what he said. Dalrymple supported the revolution that had brought William to the throne. MacKenzie did not, but neither was he committed to the Jacobites who sought the restoration of James Stuart, the previous King. His chief Seaforth was, however, a devoted Jacobite. 'Seaforth is with James in Ireland, my Lord', said MacKenzie. 'It's common knowledge. I have no time for plots. I'm done with politics. I'm happy to tend my plants and play with my grandson in my garden. I fear the revolution is a… *fait accompli*.'

Dalrymple nodded in satisfaction and sat back, observing MacKenzie carefully. He returned his quill to the stand and said smugly, 'James will never return as King of this country or any other. King William will crush the fools who support him. Your clan must accept King William. Everyone will accept King William eventually. A few clans hold out, but I will bring them into the fold… soon.'

MacKenzie smiled ruefully. 'I cannot say I'm happy with William as King. But what can I do about it? I'm too old to fight in the field. I'm content in my retirement at the Hawthorns.'

He remembered the letter that had arrived earlier from a client in the Highlands, delivered clandestinely by a MacKenzie clan agent, requesting advice on how to finance a son in exile and raise money to pay for muskets. Dalrymple would have loved to get his hands on the missive which was safely consigned to the flames of his fire.

'Why have you asked me here, my Lord?' MacKenzie asked. It was time to get down to business. Dalrymple never asked to see you for purely social reasons. 'I spend little time in the city these days. I'm thinking of selling my apartments.'

Dalrymple rested his elbows on the desk and sighed. 'Have a glass of wine, MacKenzie.' Filling two glasses from a bottle, he passed one to MacKenzie and drank deeply from the other.

'Let me explain myself. You were no doubt surprised to receive my summons this morning. We are not men who usually share the same interests. But these are unusual days. Political business consumes my time at the moment. The King, or rather his servant Portland, demands I keep him informed about Scottish policy, day and night. The secretaries are lazy and unreliable. The King's desire is to pacify Scotland and settle the church swiftly. Much business is required to achieve this end: commissioners persuaded to support the court, ministers cajoled, fanatics kept at bay. The new Crown Officer has been dismissed. He was even more useless than your dead friend Archibald Stirling. I'm too busy to concern myself with individual criminal cases.'

Dalrymple took another sip of wine, before raising his handkerchief to dab his thin, black lips. 'I want your help, MacKenzie. There, I've said it. I don't like asking any of your clan – indeed, any Highlander – for help. I've no liking for the Highlands. It's a barbarous wasteland and nursery of Popery!'

MacKenzie considered pointing out the fertility of land in Ross-shire and that only a tiny proportion of clans were Catholic, most being Protestant, but decided against it. Dalrymple was so full of Presbyterian prejudice it would make no difference.

Dalrymple continued gravely. 'There's been a killing in the city this very morning. There's been a killing in Van Diemen's Land. In a house in Cumming's Court off the Lawnmarket. A merchant called Jacob Kerr has been murdered... brutally. Dr Lawtie will provide the anatomical details. Kerr was an elder in the Kirk who sat quietly on the Session. I've no time to examine the case myself, but it must be seen to be investigated to assuage the Presbyterians.' He stopped again to drink some wine and then shook his head. 'My enemies are circling like vultures, MacKenzie.

It is jealousy of the Dalrymple family that drives them on. But mark my words. Presbytery will be re-established in Scotland. I will let nothing disrupt progress of the legislation through Parliament. I want Kerr's case investigated quickly and with little noise.'

'Surely a new Officer should consider it, my Lord', said MacKenzie, reflecting that the previous Crown Officer had lasted only a few months. Dalrymple spent long hours in the office and was often at his desk after midnight. Ordinary mortals could not put up with his demands. He lived only to work and further the interests of his family.

'I find it difficult to find a reasonable candidate', Dalrymple replied. 'Everyone is blemished in some way. Everyone represents some faction. Any appointee will displease someone. Things are carefully balanced. I don't want to upset any members of Parliament before the Kirk legislation is passed and we've raised supply. So, I need your help, MacKenzie – in an unofficial capacity, of course. I could not make you an official deputy. You are tainted by your service to the previous regime. It would ruffle too many feathers. An appointment on an ad hoc basis, however, providing authority to investigate a single case, is politically acceptable. You will, of course, be paid.'

MacKenzie took his glass and sat back, sipping the claret. 'I don't need the money, my Lord', he said.

'Consider it a way of serving the King', added Dalrymple, a wry smile spreading over his cold features. 'It would help you and your family. After all, your grandson is the son of a Papist who died on the wrong side at Killiecrankie.'

'My daughter is no Papist, my Lord.' MacKenzie had to admit it was not the best start in life for young Geordie. The boy's father was dead and would have no opinion on his son's religious upbringing, but his brother Seaforth, a staunch Catholic, might try to interfere. 'Let me think on the matter, my Lord.'

'I can give you a day, MacKenzie. I need the case tidied up now.' MacKenzie finished his wine and excused himself.

He emerged from the Parliament House into a bright June morning. He walked up the bustling High Street of Edinburgh, through the teeming Luckenbooths surrounding St Giles Kirk, towards the mass of the castle.

Business was booming after the mayhem of the last couple of years. Merchants and lawyers, who mostly followed the Presbyterian interest, were content with the new regime. William was backed by the wealthy merchants of Amsterdam and London. James faced years in exile, unless there was a miraculous turn of events in Ireland. Most Jacobites had already left for their estates in the country or joined the old King in exile; only a few of the most loyal supporters still plotted in the city.

MacKenzie shook his head in despair. Seaforth had, unsurprisingly, chosen the losing side. Fortunately, he had not committed himself one way or the other. If he had openly sided with the Jacobites, he might have faced exile and forfeiture, the Hawthorns given to some Presbyterian lackey. MacKenzie had prevaricated over providing money. The Jacobite cause was in dire need of funds. Rents from MacKenzie lands in the north were being transferred to Seaforth. The expense of maintaining the chief overseas was vast and causing disquiet among the clansfolk.

James was the rightful King of Scotland, mused MacKenzie, but he would not take up arms to restore him. In his heart, he was convinced it was over for the House of Stuart. It grieved him but they had to face reality. The Stuarts had been Kings of Scotland since Robert II, but recent members of the family had proved useless monarchs, except perhaps Charles II. Maybe Scotland should accept a future under the Dutchman William. Dalrymple was determined to crush Jacobitism in the Highlands. MacKenzie sighed.

How had it come to this? He recalled the jubilation in London on the Restoration of Charles in 1660, which he had witnessed as a young man.

MacKenzie found himself in the Lawnmarket, the part of the High Street nearest the castle, where tenements rose to seven storeys on both sides. He stood at the opening of Cockburn's Wynd, on the north side of the street, a long, narrow vennel between the tenements, leading to the courtyard of Cumming's Court about a hundred yards away. At the bottom he could see a black door. It was the front door of a five-storey dwelling, or land, called Van Diemen's Land. It was the house where Jacob Kerr had lived and died.

He knew the building was named after a Dutch merchant called Van Diemen who had built it. Van Diemen had married a Scottish woman and come to Edinburgh to trade with his homeland. He had died childless and the property had passed through a number of owners, while keeping its name.

MacKenzie knew little about Jacob Kerr except that he was a merchant of the middle rank, a Presbyterian and regular church goer. He knew nothing else about his family or business. MacKenzie had never crossed the threshold of Van Diemen's Land in his life. He turned to leave and was about to head off, dismissing Dalrymple's request, when some impulse made him look down the vennel again.

He did not have to take the case. He disliked the Dalrymple family and everything they stood for. He missed his job as Clerk of the Session. He would never return to it unless there was a miracle. But he was already wondering what had happened behind the door. It crossed his mind that Dalrymple might be using him for some purpose. But if he took the case, would he not be using Dalrymple? He had a sudden desire to be involved in an investigation again. The last few months since Geordie's birth had been delightful, but it would be good to have something else to think about. He had to admit that a murder had a magnetic pull over him.

He marched up the Lawnmarket, turned right into Merton's Close and entered the Periwig, a drinking den of advocates and writers, where he asked for ink and paper. Taking the table at the back of the low-ceilinged tavern where he usually sat, he wrote two short notes: one to Dalrymple accepting the case; the other to his friend and assistant Davie Scougall, asking him to meet him immediately in the Lawnmarket. He called a boy to deliver the messages, sat back with satisfaction and ordered a glass of claret.

CHAPTER 2

The Body of a Merchant

SCOUGALL WAS HARD at work in the office and was annoyed by the presumption of MacKenzie's request that he meet him. MacKenzie should know he no longer worked for himself. He had moved on to better things, having taken a position with Mrs Hair six months before as a senior writer. As a result, he was busier than he had ever been before and it was difficult – indeed, impossible – for him to drop everything when he worked for someone else.

Mrs Hair's business was expanding; property transactions reviving, trade finance growing strongly. Scougall was enjoying his new role. He relished meeting merchants to seal deals and was fascinated by the foreign trade. He loved to watch ships sailing from Leith to Holland or the Baltic. Despite having never been outside Scotland in his life, he had a longing to see the wider world and hoped to sail to Amsterdam or Barbados or the Indies one day. First, however, he had to prove himself to Mrs Hair.

He was sure she was pleased with his work so far. His maxim was to check every document he wrote three times: check, check and check, he would say to himself after completing a task, whether letter or bond. She had hinted he might travel to oversee her business soon. MacKenzie's note therefore came as an unwanted irritation. But he could not deny his old friend. They had been through too much together over the years. Reluctantly, he excused himself for half an hour.

On the way up the High Street he thought about Chrissie. She was no longer Chrissie Munro, but miraculously transmogrified into Chrissie Scougall. The thought of seeing her at the end of the day banished his feeling of annoyance. His married status still amazed him and brought a smile to a face which usually wore a worried expression.

Many times over the years he had thought marriage beyond his grasp. But the small ceremony in Musselburgh had taken place in April, two months before, the Reverend Andrew Leitch officiating. He still could not get used to the idea of returning to a cosy apartment rather than his lonely room in Mrs Baird's lodgings. He would have the company of a pretty woman all evening and all night. He thanked God for his good fortune and MacKenzie's words at the ceremony came back to him: 'Davie and I have survived a few scrapes over the years. I've come to know him well. He's a man of many qualities: brave, determined, indefatigable and he can drive a golf ball further than any lawyer in Edinburgh! He will make a loyal and loving husband.'

Scougall's irritation subsided. He spotted MacKenzie in the distance, a tall figure in a blue velvet coat and short wig, and for some reason thought of MacKenzie's daughter, Elizabeth. He chastised himself – thinking of another woman was a sin. He was pleased for MacKenzie that she had returned home and there was a bairn at the Hawthorns, although the child was, unfortunately, the son of a Papist. Elizabeth had left her young husband buried at Blair, and she, at the age of 22, was a very eligible widow.

MacKenzie waved in greeting from the opening of Cockburn's Wynd. 'Ah, Davie! Thank you for coming', he said excitedly.

'I've only a short while, sir. Mrs Hair does not like her writers disappearing on business unconcerned with her office', Scougall stammered, unable to conceal his anxiety.

MacKenzie smiled, taking Scougall's elbow and directing him into the vennel. 'I quite understand, Davie. I'll just take a little of your precious time. I know you're busy and keen to make a favourable impression. I've something important to tell you.' He waited for Scougall to give him his full attention before continuing. 'I've had an offer from Dalrymple.'

'An offer from Dalrymple?' Scougall repeated looking confused.

'He's offered me a criminal case to investigate. He wants it sorted with little fuss. He's too busy with parliamentary business.'

Scougall looked surprised. 'What case, sir?'

'A death in the house down there, Davie', said MacKenzie, pointing down the vennel.

Scougall looked down the dark passageway at the black door.

'Van Diemen's Land', added MacKenzie.

Scougall didn't know what to say. He knew MacKenzie hated the new government, particularly Dalrymple. 'What's it to do with me? I don't have time to assist you, sir. I'm too busy with work.'

MacKenzie rummaged in his pocket and took out his pipe. He knocked it against the wall, briskly, and began to stuff it with fresh tobacco. He was soon puffing away thoughtfully. 'If you'll allow me to explain, Davie. Jacob Kerr was found this morning in the kitchen. His body has been taken to the morgue. We should go there first.' He took hold of Scougall's sleeve and gently directed him back onto the High Street.

Scougall stopped in his tracks after a few steps, looking exasperated. 'I'm too busy, sir. I don't know if I can spare any time. I should let Mrs Hair know first. I can't be long.'

MacKenzie took the cuff of Scougall's jacket, encouraging him down the street. 'We won't be long, Davie. Tell Mrs Hair you were seeing me. You were maintaining good business relations. I require a bond to purchase land in Ross-shire. She'll be understanding, if there's money in it.'

Scougall looked perturbed but hated displeasing anyone. He had no appetite for any case of murder. He had other things to think about, in particular his work and Chrissie. But he always found it difficult to refuse MacKenzie. 'Twenty minutes and I'll have to be back in the office.'

MacKenzie set off down the High Street at a quick pace. 'Come on then, Davie. Get a move on. I'd forgotten you were working for Mrs Hair. It's very inconvenient. Could you not take your own office again? Then you might be a more... flexible assistant.' He smiled to indicate he was only half serious.

Scougall knew he was teasing him but couldn't contain his displeasure. 'I've my future to think of, sir. I'm a married man now, if you remember. I can't make a living from criminal cases like this. I don't make money like an advocate. Anyway, I enjoy my new work. It's a breath of fresh air after years of writing instruments on my own.'

MacKenzie chuckled. 'Of course, Davie, forgive me. You can help me as your time permits. I'm sorry for my presumption. I've grown too used to your help. A second opinion is important to me. The thought of a new case has sent the blood pumping through my old veins. It's been a long time since I had something to get my teeth into. I was going to decline the case, of course, on a matter of principle. I despise Dalrymple's clique of craven Calvinists. He's no friend of Highlanders, especially MacKenzies. But I've decided to lay my prejudices aside, on this occasion. I have an aching desire in me to be involved. It's no doubt a botched robbery which should be solved quickly.'

They had reached the Tolbooth, the sprawling lump of stone at the centre of the city beside St Giles Kirk used as a prison, morgue, council chamber and headquarters of the town guard. 'A quick look at the body and I'll leave you to get on with your work. I promise, Davie', added MacKenzie as they entered the low door and headed down a staircase into the basement.

The morgue was the first room on the left, a long, low-ceilinged chamber containing a line of wooden tables. Inside, Dr Lawtie, a small flabby figure wearing spectacles, was explaining the best way to cut open a cadaver to an apprentice. Lawtie was also annoyed at being interrupted.

'You again, MacKenzie. And Mr Scougall', he said bluntly. Lawtie disliked lawyers and showed it.

'I'm looking into the Kerr killing for Dalrymple. Is that him there?' MacKenzie pointed at the only table with anything on it – a large mound under a white sheet.

'You'll work for anyone! I thought you were a Jacobite', replied Lawtie, wiping his hands on his blood-stained apron.

'Then you thought wrongly, Lawtie. I'm no Jacobite, nor am I a Williamite, as they call supporters of the new King. I'm a loyal Scotsman. May we take a look at him?' MacKenzie pulled back the sheet before Lawtie gave his approval.

A grotesque mound of blue-white, blubbery flesh was revealed. Scougall recalled the whale he had seen as a boy washed up on the beach at Musselburgh. Kerr was a gross middle-aged man who was bald as a coot with a plethora of varicosities on his legs.

'He was a big man', said Lawtie. 'He must weigh... 20 stones at least. It took four guards to carry him down here. We struggled to turn him to examine the wounds on his back.'

'How was he killed?' asked MacKenzie brusquely, observing the corpse carefully.

'Let me show you, MacKenzie.'

Lawtie called his assistant, a young man of about 15 who looked terrified of his master. Together, they took hold of the body and with some effort tipped it onto its side and held it there, revealing a vast pimpled back punctured by a random array of small stab wounds.

'I've counted 20 wounds in total. Both lungs are punctured, the heart is pierced thrice, the main vessels around the heart slashed. It was a frenzied attack. And look at the neck. It was cut as well.'

'Did he die from the neck wound or the ones on the back?' asked MacKenzie, moving closer to observe the lacerations.

'The neck wound caused his death. But the others would have killed him in time.'

'What kind of weapon was used?'

'Anything with a blade. A dirk or kitchen knife. I would judge a relatively small one from the depth of the wounds. It was wielded ferociously. There's one thing about the angle of incision. The stabs were made downwards.'

'Was he lying on his back at the time?' asked Scougall, standing as far away from the corpse as he could – he had an aversion to dead bodies but his interest in the details of the killing was suddenly pricked.

'No, I would say not, Mr Scougall. Rather, the killer brought the weapon down like this.' Lawtie suddenly pushed his surprised assistant to the floor and indicated with his fist a stabbing motion onto his back. 'Now, get up off the floor, Munro!' he barked.

'Is there anything else of note?' probed MacKenzie.

Lawtie took a handkerchief from his pocket and blew his bulbous nose. 'There is one other thing. There are a number of lesions on his member. Old ones, I think. Probably caused by a venereal complaint in the past.'

Scougall looked baffled and repeated, 'Lesions on his member?'

'The clap, Mr Scougall. Kerr suffered from the clap. A case of gonorrhoea. They are long healed. He probably visited a whore or two in his youth.'

'I thought Kerr was an elder in the Kirk?' asked Scougall, disappointed by another example of the moral failings of those espousing the cause of rectitude.

MacKenzie nodded as he took a pair of tweezers from his pocket and lifted Kerr's flaccid penis from its nest of grey hair to examine it. Scougall looked away in disgust. He also had an aversion to looking at another man's penis, particularly a dead man's.

'He strayed a little in his youth! Who has not strayed a little in their youth, Mr Scougall? Who has not been tempted?' Lawtie chuckled, sensing Scougall's discomfiture.

The repulsive thought of Lawtie astride a poor woman flashed through Scougall's mind. Was the good doctor married? He did not know. He had never thought of it before. That Lawtie should have a life, a sex life, outside the disgusting morgue where he spent his days had never entered Scougall's mind. He had always wanted to escape his company as quickly as possible. He pitied any woman forced to share a bed with the disgusting little man. Then a thought of himself and Chrissie came from nowhere. It was not right to think of their love making in such a place, in a morgue, in a place of death. He forced himself to think of something else by following the blue varicosities on Kerr's swollen legs which reminded him of the tributaries of a river on a Blaeu map.

'What was he wearing when he was killed?' asked MacKenzie.

'Just his nightshirt and leather belt', replied Lawtie. 'A pouch attached to it contained a few coins. They are over there on the table. I had to cut the nightshirt off to look at the wounds. Nothing else on it but blood, lots of blood. The pouch is there.'

'I must get back to the office, sir', said Scougall, backing away from the corpse, beginning to feel queasy. He hated the putrid reek and closeness of death. He turned his eyes away from the long, curving yellow toenails of Kerr's reptilian feet.

MacKenzie who was deep in thought nodded absently. 'Thank you, Davie. A drink later in the Periwig? To keep you informed about the case.'

Scougall nodded, unenthusiastically. Chrissie would not mind him taking a glass or two. She thought well of MacKenzie. But he could not stop feeling dismayed by it all. He wanted to get on with his new life.

CHAPTER 3

Van Diemen's Land

MACKENZIE RETURNED TO Dalrymple's office immediately to pick up a letter drafted by one of the Advocate's clerks which affirmed his appointment as a temporary deputy for the space of a week. The period of time might be extended if required.

Stuffing it in his pocket, he returned to the entrance of Cockburn's Wynd on the High Street where he stood, once more deep in thought, staring down the narrow passageway at the door of Van Diemen's Land, trying to remember everything he knew about Kerr. The details provided by Dalrymple were sparse. Kerr was born about 50 years ago, his father a merchant and his mother the daughter of a merchant. He had followed his father's trade from a young age. He married Margaret Petrie, the daughter of Alexander Petrie, another merchant; they had one child, a daughter Mary, a quiet devout girl. Kerr, it seems, had bothered no one during his life until that morning when Van Diemen's Land was visited by brutal violence. An aphorism in Gaelic, MacKenzie's first language, came to him, about how death comes suddenly like an unexpected summer storm.

He recalled his wife's smiling face in the gardens at the Hawthorns a few days before her death in childbirth and felt the usual anguish, the familiar feeling of despair he had fought against for 20 years. But the vision of his wife faded and was replaced by his grandson squealing in laughter. The boy was the apple of his eye. How his wife would have loved to see their grandchild. He suddenly reflected that Geordie was not being brought up speaking Gaelic. His daughter was talking to him entirely in English. He shook his head in disgust and resolved to rectify the matter as soon as he got back to the Hawthorns.

He walked down the vennel ponderously, listening to his own footsteps, observing the damp stone of the walls of the tenements on both sides, noticing how they leaned together as they rose storey after storey until, seven storeys above, they were little more than a couple of feet apart and only a thin rectangle of blue sky was visible. It was like walking through a long, peaked cave.

Another thing struck him as he proceeded. The vennel was relatively free of clart by Edinburgh standards. Most closes, vennels and wynds in the city hit the nose immediately on entry due to the mixture of ordure and shit dumped from the windows above. Cockburn's Wynd was clear of the usual detritus and looked like it was regularly swept. It was a well-ordered corner in the chaos of the city.

At the bottom, he entered a small courtyard, Cumming's Court, also kept clean, around which a number of tenements, or lands, were built. On the north side, Henderson's Land and Van Diemen's Land conjoined, each the mirror image of the other, with Cunningham's Land on the east and Learmonth's Land on the west. To the south, a high wall obscured the rigs of the buildings on the High Street. Two tiny passageways on the sides of Henderson's Land and Van Diemen's Land led north to the rear of the buildings and their rigs, and then to an overgrown slope that dropped steeply to the Nor Loch, the area of stagnant water and marsh on the north of Edinburgh that had acted as a defensive barrier over the centuries.

It was a fine, cloudless day but little sunlight warmed the cobbles in the courtyard because of shadows cast by the tenements. It was a forgotten corner of the city that

MacKenzie had hardly ever passed through, despite living in Edinburgh for most of his adult life. Perhaps he had staggered down the vennel after a late-night drinking session as a young advocate but he had never visited any of the houses in the courtyard.

MacKenzie stood before the door of Van Diemen's Land. Apart from its exotic name, there was little out of the ordinary about the house. It was a typical merchant's dwelling of five storeys and a basement, narrow and tall with crow-stepped gables in the Dutch style. His eyes took in the sash windows on each floor, clean and well-attended. The lintel above the door was carved with the coat of arms of Van Diemen and gave the year of the building's construction as 1627. He calculated for a moment. Van Diemen's Land was 63 years old, eight years older than he was. It was in a good state of repair. The door was spotless and freshly painted in black; the stonework well-pointed. It was a tidy dwelling place, exhibiting order and the wealth of its dead owner.

It was such an ordinary Edinburgh scene – a merchant's dwelling house off the High Street. He could hear the distant hum of the Lawnmarket – merchants, tradesmen, artisans, street boys going about their business. He hesitated to knock on the door. Everything appeared calm from outside in the courtyard but once he passed through the threshold, not as a friend of the house but investigator of a killing, things might not be so serene. He would have to ask uncomfortable questions of those who lived behind that door. But he was used to such things after a lifetime in the law and he relished a bit of trouble.

An image of Kerr's scarred penis flashed through his mind. What kind of man was this devout merchant? He was surely not as holy as he appeared in public. A slither of excitement passed through MacKenzie. You never knew what you might find when investigating a murder. He knocked firmly on the door.

A maid servant answered after a minute. She stood silently, soberly dressed in a black frock and white mutch, looking up at him with a pretty face. 'I'm here to see Mrs Kerr, my dear. I am John MacKenzie, advocate. I've been sent by Dalrymple. Lord Advocate Dalrymple. It's about the death of your master.'

She nodded vacantly, her expression showing little sign of grief. 'Come in, sir', she said in a soft voice.

He followed her down a passageway and up a flight of stairs. The sense of order he had noticed outside continued inside the house. Everything was clean and tidy. He passed a room on the right packed full of bales of cloth where it seemed Kerr had attended to his business. They climbed the turnpike stairway at the back of the house. MacKenzie observed the staircase going down to another floor beneath. The kitchen, where the body had been found, was down there. He had a quick look on the stairs for anything, but it looked well-scrubbed. They continued the climb up to the first floor. The maid crossed the hallway to enter a door and said something inside he could not hear. She beckoned him to enter, closing the door after him but remaining outside.

MacKenzie found himself in the living chamber of Van Diemen's Land, a large room with two sash windows overlooking the courtyard at the front of the house, comfortably furnished with finely embroidered armchairs, wooden tables and cabinets. The walls were covered in wood-panelling and paintings. Despite it being summer, a fire burned in the hearth. The chamber exuded comfort, status and wealth. A woman dressed in black stood at the window with her back to the door, looking down on the courtyard.

When she turned, MacKenzie realised it must be Mrs Kerr, the deceased merchant's wife. A middle-aged woman simply dressed in a long black frock, with a distraught expression and tears on her cheeks. She rubbed her hands on her skirt in an agitated way as she came closer and gave him her hand.

'I'm sorry for your loss, madam. So sudden. You'll be in a state of shock', said MacKenzie, noticing the look of exhaustion on her face, but also a glimmer of beauty through the veneer of anguish.

She tried to smile but began to sob, and for a few moments stood crying in the middle of the room, until she was helped by MacKenzie into a plush chair. He sat on the one opposite her and waited for a few moments, allowing her to gather herself.

'I cannot believe it, Mr MacKenzie', she said. 'He's gone... gone... it's over... our life together here... all over... 20 years of marriage... finished, complete. I'll never see him again... I'll never see him again in this world... but maybe with God's grace in the next one... when we are both cleansed of our sins. We may meet again in the love of Christ.' She took a lace handkerchief and wiped her eyes, before continuing. 'I'm sorry you see me in this state of distress, sir. Last night all was well in this house. Last night we were protected by the Lord. Today the world is transformed. Everything is changed in a matter of hours.'

MacKenzie nodded sympathetically. 'A death is like a summer storm, as we say in Gaelic, madam. It comes from nowhere and shakes the foundations of our world. I've been sent by Dalrymple.' He took the crumpled paper authorising his appointment from his pocket and held it out but she showed no interest in it. 'He wants me to investigate the killing of your husband', he added.

There was a knock on the door. The same maid entered carrying a tray which she set down on a table beside them. On it was a bottle of wine, two glasses and a plate of sweetmeats. The maid said nothing and left the room.

MacKenzie turned to Mrs Kerr and observed her carefully as she settled herself. She looked almost manic in her grief with a deathly pale face. 'I know this will be hard for you so soon after his death, Mrs Kerr', he began. 'But I must ask a few questions. I must also examine the kitchen for myself.'

She nodded, hesitantly, coming back to herself from far away. 'It's not your fault, Mr MacKenzie.' She clasped her hands in her lap and tried to compose herself, pulling her knees together and holding the tips of her fingers together as if she was about to pray, but the sobs kept coming intermittently.

MacKenzie had a sudden desire to smoke and sought his pipe in his pocket. But he reflected it would be disrespectful and took his hand out again. 'Could you tell me what happened? Begin with last night, madam. Take your time. Tell me everything you remember.'

She turned to look out the window as she spoke, as if gazing off into another world. 'My husband locked up the house with Thomas at eight o'clock as usual. He followed the same routine every night. All the doors and windows on the first three storeys were secured. I went to bed about nine. My husband remained in his office afterwards. I heard him coming to bed at some point in the night. I know not what hour it was. I was roused briefly from my sleep when he got into bed. He must have got up again later but I did not hear him go out of our chamber. It must have been some time during the hours of darkness.

'When I woke in the morning with the dawn, he was not in bed. I was not worried. It was not unusual. He often rose before me if he had to be at the markets or down in Leith. I rose from bed. Then, as I was dressing, I heard screams downstairs. I left my room immediately and met Mary, my daughter, on the landing. She had just come out of her room, having also heard the screams. We went down to the kitchen together. At first, I thought something had happened to Agnes or perhaps the boy, Thomas. I did not think it could be anything to do with my husband. But Jacob was lying on the kitchen floor. There was blood everywhere!'

She turned back to face MacKenzie with an expression of horror. 'I've never seen so much blood! A pool on the floor around him, as if all of his blood had seeped out of his body! I tried to rouse him. But he would not stir. I tried to bring him back to this world. I begged him to return to us. But when I touched him, he was cold as stone on a winter's day. He was already gone to the next world. I told Mary to return to her chamber and stay there, and Jane, our maid, who had come down also, to run and fetch the Guard. Two of them came a little later, and then another two had to be fetched to carry him to the morgue.'

MacKenzie listened patiently, then asked, 'Did you notice a weapon on the floor near him or elsewhere in the kitchen. Was there anything disturbed in the kitchen?'

She paused for a moment before replying, 'I don't think so but I wasn't thinking straight at the time. I don't remember seeing anything near the body. Perhaps Agnes, our cook, will know if an implement is missing from the kitchen or a weapon found there.'

'Did your husband carry a weapon himself, madam?' asked MacKenzie.

She shook her head. 'Never, although there's a gun in one of the kists. I cannot remember him ever taking it out.'

MacKenzie leaned forward to pour the wine. He handed her a glass, which she refused. He poured one for himself and took a sip, noting it was fine claret. 'Who lives in Van Diemen's Land with you, madam?' He sought a notebook and pencil from his pocket and reflected that Davie Scougall usually took notes for him.

'There were six of us, including my husband. So five now', she sighed. 'My daughter Mary. Our maid Jane, who just served us. Our cook Agnes and her son Thomas. We are a small household. We were a contented household. We lived quietly following the word of God.' She paused for a second and then continued, with a quizzical expression. 'I do not understand why the Lord has allowed this to happen to us.' She emphasised the last word. 'Why would He punish us and allow sinners to prosper in this world?' she asked blankly, not directing her question at MacKenzie, but as if someone else stood beside the window.

'Your husband was an elder in the Kirk, madam?' MacKenzie continued to question her in a perfunctory manner.

'He was a godly and devout man. He served on the Session for many years. After attending church on the Sabbath, he would pray for hours in the house. He devoted his life to the Lord.'

'Is there any sign of forced entry to the house?'

'I do not know, sir. I have not looked round the doors yet. I never thought to do so.'

MacKenzie smiled. 'I will examine them in turn. Do you know if anything has been taken from the house – any of your husband's goods or money?'

She shook her head briskly again. 'I can think of nothing obvious that is missing. I'll check my jewels and our plate presently. I have not looked at the stock. We have some expensive pieces of cloth but I do not know how much. I know not if the kists have been touched. They are in the office off the chamber on the ground floor.'

MacKenzie sat back in his chair and finished the glass, savouring the fine wine. Kerr had a good cellar for an elder of the Kirk. He thought about pouring himself a second glass, but decided it would be impolite. It was indeed a nuisance that Scougall could not help him; his shorthand skills were useful. He would have to do with a few cursory notes and rely on his memory which was not as good as it used to be. 'Can you think of anyone who might want to harm your husband, Mrs Kerr?' he asked. 'Did he have any enemies?'

She shook her head. 'I cannot think of any, sir. He was a godly man in his affairs who believed in a fair deal for his customers. That's what he always said. He was not grasping after profit like some merchants in this city.'

'What about his role as elder in the Kirk Session?' MacKenzie despised the sanctimonious hypocrites on the Session who judged the sins of others. He feared their power would rise once presbytery was sanctioned by Parliament. The puritans would be back in charge like the days of Cromwell. They would soon be banning Christmas and anything that smacked of pleasure.

'He was a quiet man in the Session', she replied. 'He did not rail against sin like some. He was not a… he was not a fanatic. He served the Lord in a restrained manner, in a moderate way. He was not one of the hot-heads in the Kirk.'

MacKenzie nodded, thoughtfully. There were enough hot-heads in Scotland. Kerr sounded like a solid, dull Presbyterian. The Tron Kirk Bell began to chime in the distance on the High Street. He sat watching her and waited until it had rung 11 times. 'Tell me about yourself, madam. Where do you hail from, when you married Mr Kerr.'

She looked up at him with a sharper expression. 'Is it necessary, sir? At such a time to talk on my own history seems disrespectful to the memory of my husband.'

'I assure you it is necessary, madam. I'm experienced in such matters. I'm experienced in the matter of murder. I need to know as much as possible about all those who live in Van Diemen's Land. It may help to find your husband's killer. I would not ask you if I did not think it might help.'

She sighed then continued. 'I was born in Edinburgh. I am the daughter of Alexander Petrie. My mother and father are long dead. I married Jacob 20 years ago when I was just a girl, really, only 16 at the time. The match was arranged by our families. The first years were hard ones as Jacob established his business. We did not have much money and we lived in a tiny apartment in Cochrane's Land. We worked hard and prayed hard and God shone his light on us. He let us build up a flourishing trade. It has allowed us some ease in recent years. We bought this house a dozen years ago. We could just afford it then. But look around you. We have all the trappings of worldly wealth. We have books, paintings, plate. But we are not ostentatious like some folk. We could have a coach and horses but we do not keep one. We are restrained in our spending. We live moderately in the service of the Lord. I thought we were rich in body and soul. So why doth the Lord punish us now?' Her head dropped and she began to sob again into her handkerchief.

MacKenzie was silent for a few moments, waiting for the grief to wash through her, but ignored her question when he continued with his. 'What can you tell me about your husband's history?'

She shook her head again, looking aggrieved. 'There's not much else to say. He was born in Edinburgh in 1640. He attended the burgh school and followed his father's profession of merchant. He worked hard every day of his life. He served the Lord every day of his life. He led an exemplary life. Everyone said so.'

The image of Kerr's penis again appeared in MacKenzie's mind. Kerr was not as holy as everyone thought. Did she know anything of his other history? Surely as his wife of 20 years she would have some inkling about his less sacred desires. 'How old is your daughter, madam?' he asked.

'Eighteen years.'

'You have no other children?'

'No, sir.' She hesitated for a moment before continuing, reluctantly. 'I have miscarried many times. Some almost carried to full term. The Lord has provided us with only one healthy child. We are thankful for her. She is my... life...'

'I'm sorry for your losses, madam.' MacKenzie thought of his own grandchild. A memory from a few months before struck him powerfully. He was waiting for the birth at the Hawthorns, taking refuge in whisky, listening desperately as the midwife tried to comfort his daughter in the room upstairs. He had prayed fervently to God in those moments, the God he did not believe in, that she would not be taken from him like his wife. Thankfully, all had ended well. The bairn was strong and Elizabeth did not bleed too much. He was certainly content with just one grandchild. He could never tell Elizabeth he prayed she would never marry again, so she would not have to risk another birth. Geordie's father Ruairidh, who had died on the battlefield of Killiecrankie, was already being praised as a Jacobite hero in Gaelic songs. The truth was he was a pathetic creature. But like many wretches who fell in war, he was elevated in death. Elizabeth must've seen some good in him, but he could not see what it was. 'I'll take in the house now, Mrs Kerr', he said, rising stiffly to his feet. 'I'll start with the kitchen.'

'I cannot join you just now, Mr MacKenzie. I must attend my daughter. Please look round yourself. You have my permission to go anywhere.'

MacKenzie left the chamber and crossed the hallway to the turnpike stairs at the back of the house. He descended slowly to the ground floor, then continued down another flight to the basement, examining the stairs closely for any hint of blood. They were all scrubbed and swept clean. At the bottom, the stairway opened into a short corridor which led into the kitchen, a large, low-ceilinged room, encompassing most of the bottom of the tenement. The first thing to catch his eye was a large dark stain on the floor beside the table. Further stains ended abruptly where the kitchen became the corridor. The floor of the corridor had been washed but the kitchen floor had not. MacKenzie stood at the bottom of the stairs for a few moments, surveying the scene.

A long wooden table filled the middle of the kitchen, covered in cooking utensils and bowls and pans. They all looked clean and ready for the day's cooking. There were a few chairs around the table but one was turned towards the stairs. On the right side was a small larder and on the left a long, black range. Another door beyond the range probably led to a laundry. He moved forward and looked down at the floor around the table. It was obvious where Kerr's body had lain from the bloodstains and numerous footprints leading from them. Four guards had carried the body back to the Tolbooth. They had left a confusing mess behind. He got down on his haunches near the main stain, his head at table height. There was evidence of blood almost everywhere: flecks on the table legs, the underside of a large wooden bowl on the table and on other cooking utensils. An image came to him of a flashing blade being driven into Kerr's back, splattering blood everywhere. The body had been lifted away only a few hours before. Here in the kitchen, Kerr was stabbed 20 times in the back. The knife was wielded savagely in a frenzied attack. He looked under the table, noticing a few hairs caught between the planks on the underside of the tabletop. Down beside the leg of the table on the floor was a small clump of hair matted together by coagulated blood. Someone had been under the table, perhaps the boy. But was it left there last night or before? He pulled out a few of the hairs from the table and then picked up the clump, placing them all in a piece of cloth he carried in his pocket.

He rose to his feet and stretched his back, before moving carefully round the main blood stain. He went to the back wall on the north side of the house and examined a line of kitchen knives in a wooden rack on a table beside a stone sink. Any one of them might have been the murder weapon, although one was missing from the holder. He took a knife and tested it on his thumb. It was sharp enough to puncture Kerr's heart. He took each one out individually and examined their blades. They were all scrubbed clean, as was the table and the sink. The weapon might have been washed after the attack and replaced on the rack. That was unlikely if the killer was a thief. Or was the missing knife taken away by the killer?

He tried the window above the sink. It was secured with crossed bars of iron. No one could gain access there. Had Kerr simply disturbed a burglar? But something felt wrong with that interpretation. The frenzy of the attack pointed to something else. Perhaps the killer bore a grudge against the merchant. A disturbed thief would have stabbed him once or twice, then run away. And there was another fact to consider. Kerr was a large man – how was he stabbed 20 times in the back without fighting back? He must have made his own way to the kitchen. It was impossible to conceive he was killed somewhere else and moved without a small army to shift him.

MacKenzie entered the larder on the right side of the kitchen and was struck by the rich reek inside. His eyes darted round the contents of the room: small barrels of barley, herring and meal, large cheeses and sugar loaves, dishes of prunes, raisins and currants. There were two wooden chests on the floor, one containing loaves of bread, the other candles. He checked behind the cheeses and hams on the shelves and got down on the floor to look behind some bags of flour.

The other door on the left opened into a small laundry. It contained a wooden table on which a pile of ironed clothes was neatly placed beside a couple of irons. The room also contained a metal mangle and large laundry basket. MacKenzie rummaged through the soiled linen. There were just a couple of shirts and a few pairs of undergarments, but no sign of blood on any of them.

He returned to the kitchen and examined the range. Had something been burned there in the night? He took a rag and opened the small metal door, peering inside. It had burned out and was full of ash. A small white shape caught his eye at the front. He picked it up delicately. It was a small fragment of material, a couple of inches in length, partly burned. He placed it in his pocket and stood for a few moments more, contemplating the scene, recalling the kitchen of his foster mother years before when he was a boy in the Highlands. It had been his job to make sure the range was supplied with a plentiful supply of peat. He had taken a particular pleasure in the responsibility, carrying the basket back and forward from the peat stack. He remembered the sweet odour of burning peat filling the house. The range in Van Diemen's Land used coal. A scuttle sat beside it. He picked up a lump of coal and stared at it, before dropping it back into the scuttle.

On the way out the kitchen, MacKenzie cleaned his shoes with the rag to remove any blood picked up from the floor. He climbed the stairs to the ground floor and walked down the narrow hall to check the front door. It was bolted securely and the lock appeared sound. He turned into Kerr's trading premises on the right, a large bright room full of bales of cloth which included calico, blue linen, brown linen, diaper, serge and Yorkshire. A fine bale of green linen and some high-quality muslin caught his eye. Kerr must have had rich customers.

The window at the front of the chamber which looked out on the courtyard was made up of dozens of tiny rhomboid panes of glass. They were all intact. Another window at the back of the chamber looked out onto the rig behind and there was a door to the garden. The window was also barred with iron and intact. MacKenzie entered the office on the left. It had one tiny window, high on the wall which was too small for anyone to enter through. Inside the office, documents and papers were strewn over the floor and the desk had been ransacked.

There were two kists on the floor. The lid of the smaller one was open. MacKenzie got down on his haunches. A key, part of a set, was in the lock and the kist was empty. He turned to the larger kist and found it was locked. He tried to move it along the floor, but it would not budge more than a few inches because it was chained to the wall. He took the set of keys from the lock of the small kist. The second one fitted and he opened the larger one. Inside was a pile of bonds, notes and bills of exchange. Underneath the stack of paper, he found a pistol, as well as gold and silver coins, guineas and pieces of eight. He quickly estimated they came to a healthy sum – a couple of hundred pounds sterling at least. The burglar had chosen the wrong kist.

MacKenzie returned to the back door and noticed it was very slightly ajar. He pulled it open carefully. It provided access to a stone platform above the basement which led to the yard at the back. It was immediately obvious the lock had been broken. A vision flashed through his mind of the killer entering here, but why did he or she descend into the kitchen? If Kerr had disturbed a thief, he would have confronted the person up here. Or had the thief taken Kerr down to the kitchen for some reason? He closed the door gently and returned to the office to examine the debris on the floor more carefully. Letters and lists lay everywhere. He picked up a random paper – an inventory of cloth Kerr had bought in Amsterdam.

He noticed a line of ledgers on a shelf above the desk. He looked through the first fat leather-bound volume. The ledger itemised Kerr's purchases and sales back in the 1670s. MacKenzie returned it and took the next on the right. The book was only half used. He found a number of transactions dated the day before – three in total. He wrote the names in his notebook. William Spence, Ninian Reid and Archibald Purves were all tailors in Edinburgh. A portrait of Kerr and his wife on the wall opposite the window caught his attention. The painting gave the impression of confidence and wealth, but there was something about the demeanour of Margaret Kerr. MacKenzie noticed again that she was a fine-looking woman, if a serious one. From the picture she hardly appeared a happy wife. A knock on the door startled him. Margaret Kerr herself stood at the doorway; the same beautiful, unhappy face in the painting, although a little older.

She spoke first. 'Was the motive theft, Mr MacKenzie? I see the back door has been broken.'

'It's too early to say, madam', replied MacKenzie.

She moved into the room and looked at the kists. 'My husband always carried the keys with him. Everything is gone from the smaller one.'

'It may be burglary', replied MacKenzie, nodding. 'But I haven't seen around the house yet. Where did your husband keep his keys?'

'They were always on his belt. He wore his belt even in bed at night. He never took it off.' She crossed her arms over her chest and looked away.

MacKenzie moved closer to her. 'Do you know what's been taken from here?'

'The cash was kept in the larger one. The small one contained items concerned with daily business. Maybe some bonds... correspondence, that kind of thing, a little petty cash perhaps. He kept important things in the larger one.'

'Why would a thief take the papers from the small kist and not try to open the larger one?' asked MacKenzie. She did not reply and shook her head. MacKenzie turned back to the portrait, smiling. 'A fine likeness. When was it painted, madam?'

She stood transfixed for a few moments staring at the image, before coming back to herself. 'About ten years ago. A Dutch artist was in town painting nobles and lawyers and merchants. It cost us a pretty packet. Jacob was adamant we should be recorded for posterity. The artist was impressed by the Dutch name of our house. He was disappointed to learn we did not belong to the original family.'

MacKenzie smiled. 'Is it a good likeness of your husband?'

She looked at the painting again, and as she did so, dropped to her knees. She cried out, 'What are we to do now, sir? Why has God forsaken us? Why has He taken him?'

MacKenzie helped her back to her feet. As she looked up at him, he saw for an instant the younger woman in the portrait. She was bonnie indeed, if a tad severe, like many Scottish lasses. The ministers and elders of the Kirk, like her husband, demanded their wives dress like crows. He looked again at the portrait. Kerr appeared confident to the point of arrogant with a large belly protruding over his belt. And there were the keys hanging from it. The keys he slept with. The security of his house and the kists was paramount to him as a merchant. MacKenzie observed Kerr's large florid cheeks, cold eyes and double chin. Something made MacKenzie shudder at the owner of Van Diemen's Land.

He turned from the painting and nodded at Mrs Kerr. 'I'll take in the rest of the house myself, madam.'

She stood back to let him pass. 'I must rest, sir. I'm exhausted. Tell me when you're finished.'

MacKenzie went to the back door again and examined the lock carefully. Debris had fallen onto the floor. The marks on the wood around the lock suggested a tool was used to force it. He pulled the door further open to look at the lock on both sides of the door, allowing in fresh air, a slight breeze from the north. He inspected the stone platform outside for any footprints but could not find any. It had been dry overnight, he reflected. Once over the platform, a narrow path led through the rig to a low wall. Beyond there was thick vegetation and a grassy slope descending to the Nor Loch.

Walking down the rig, he looked for footprints among the vegetables and flowers of the well-attended garden. He was struck by a desire to be back in his own gardens at the Hawthorns which he had neglected recently. He stood at the low wall at the bottom of the rig. A narrow path ran along the other side which could be accessed from the passageway on the eastern side of Van Diemen's Land and the one on the western side of the tenement attached to it. He stood for a while looking down the slope, before turning and observing the back of Van Diemen's Land. All appeared in order there too.

He retraced his steps to the platform and re-entered the house, closing the door behind him. He went up the stairway to the first floor and entered the living chamber again. He was surprised to see Mrs Kerr in the room. She had not returned to her bed chamber as she had said. Instead, she sat with a Bible on her lap, with head bowed and eyes closed, an expression of intensity on her face as she prayed.

A young, painfully thin woman in a black frock with a white bonnet on her head – he presumed it was her daughter Mary – was sitting on the floor at her feet, her back pressed against her mother's legs. He introduced himself to her.

Mary's skeletal face nodded a timid greeting. Her eyes dropped as soon as he looked at her.

He then went to the windows looking down on the courtyard. Both were securely fastened. He went to the fire. The position of the chamber meant that there was little sunlight to warm the room. He could see nothing of interest in or around the hearth.

Excusing himself, he returned to the hall and entered the only other room on the floor. A large wooden table and six finely upholstered chairs suggested it was the Kerr's dining room. An ornately carved wooden sideboard contained an impressive collection of silver and pewter plate. The thief could have made a packet by stealing it but the room had been left undisturbed. MacKenzie moved his finger across the top of the table. It was covered in a fine layer of dust. The family had not dined in the chamber for a while. He went to the window looking down on the Nor Loch beneath. The room was at the rear of the house, giving a pleasant view of the grey Firth and rich lands of Fife beyond. It was a peaceful scene on a fine summer's day. A landscape artist could have made a pretty painting of it.

MacKenzie turned to survey the room; everything was calm and restrained, almost like a painting by a Dutch master. But the canvas had been torn asunder that morning by an act of extreme violence. He reflected that the chamber had a much better view than his own dining room in Libberton's Wynd which was on the other side of the High Street and looked south towards the Pentland Hills. As he stood, he felt strangely extruded from the normal world of the city and he let his mind drift from the case for a few moments. Elizabeth was no longer in the Highlands with an army, that particular nightmare was over. She was with her bairn at the Hawthorns and both were in good health. The thought cheered him despite the atmosphere in the house. He would get the case sorted quickly and return to the Hawthorns as soon as he could. He was struck by an overwhelming desire to see his grandson, recalling fondly his dark, curly locks and infectious laugh. He would write to Elizabeth later that day explaining why he would be away for a couple more days. He knew she would not be pleased.

He went upstairs to the second floor, examining the staircase carefully. Again, there was nothing. There were two rooms on this floor as well. The one on the front was the main bedchamber, which belonged to Kerr and his wife. He knocked on the door in case someone was inside and, when there was no reply, entered the room. It was the same size as the living chamber beneath, although the whitewashed ceiling was slightly lower. A generous four-poster bed stood at one side of the room with small tables on each side of it; on the other wall, dark wooden presses and a single bookcase. He took out a few of the titles and leafed through them, shaking his head at the subject matter of Presbyterian religious devotion. Scougall would no doubt approve! The reading habits of an elder were as dry as dust! On each table sat a ponderous Bible, one for him and one for her.

He went to the presses. There were clothes for him and her inside both, sober, restrained, well-tailored, black suits and dresses, with white shirts and laundered nightshirts. The wooden floorboards were scrubbed clean. One of the windows was opened slightly to air the room. It was too high to climb up to gain access.

He went back to the bed and looked down on it. A vision of Kerr's bulk on top of his pretty wife flashed through his mind. He pulled back the sheets and looked under them and the pillows, but found nothing. He re-made the bed as best he could, although it had lost something of its pristineness. He looked under it. Two chamber pots, one for him and one for her. Another image flashed through his mind – Kerr stooping to urinate in the middle of the night. One had been emptied, the other not, no doubt forgotten in the morning's chaos. Some of the piss was spilt on the floor beside the full one. He wondered if the yellow liquid was Kerr's or his wife's. Perhaps a last piss before he met his maker. Another Gaelic aphorism came to him describing how the wise man remembered to empty his own chamber pot and he smiled to himself.

He went back into the hall. A knock on the other door and he entered the other room. It was slightly smaller but furnished in the same manner, almost an exact copy of the larger bedroom. A Bible rested on the bedside table beside another couple of books. A small bookcase contained the same reading material, published letters and printed sermons of the divines of the Scottish Kirk. The single window was open, providing the same view to the north as the dining room beneath. This must be Mary Kerr's chamber, the daughter of the house. It was a life scrubbed clean of unnecessary things, the puritan's chamber of contemplation, a place of prayer and sleep. She would be rewarded in the next life for restraint in this, while condemning everyone else to eternal damnation for enjoying themselves. Such was the insane logic of the doctrine of predestination. MacKenzie shook his head in disgust.

He went back to the stairs and climbed up to the third floor. The stairway narrowed and the ceiling was lower again, marking the decline in status of the occupants of the two rooms. He knocked and entered the one to the front. It was sparsely furnished with poorer quality furniture, although still comfortable enough. No Bibles, no books, only a few wooden toys on the floor. It must belong to Agnes and Thomas. MacKenzie got down on his knees and picked up a crudely carved wooden soldier, painted red and blue. He looked carefully behind each piece of furniture, as he had done in the other rooms. The press contained a few pieces of plain clothing. Under the pillows were nightshirts, neatly folded. The chamber pots under the bed were empty.

He went to the other smaller chamber. It must be the maid Jane's. It contained only a small bed, press, table and a single chair at the window. A few books in a tiny bookcase, made of planks balanced together, contained the same devotional literature. He picked one out and opened it. To his surprise, it was annotated in a neat hand. Comments about the text filled every margin. He read a few of them. Jane clearly had a sharp intelligence. The marginalia questioned every point of theology, except her own blind faith. A couple of simple black skirts hung in the press and there was a laundered nightdress, folded pristinely. She had few possessions, but more than most maids. A couple of simple pieces of jewellery lay on the table, a brooch and necklace. Her bed was made to precision. There was nothing under the pillow or under the bed except an empty chamber pot. She lived simply but in some comfort for a servant.

MacKenzie followed the stairs up to the garret at the top of the house where other servants would have slept if the Kerrs had a larger household. He had to lower his head as the ceiling was only about five and a half feet above the floor in the small hallway at the top of the stairs, which led into a long, narrow chamber. It looked like it was used as a storeroom, although there was not much stored in it, except a few boxes and the frame of an old bed. He rummaged in the boxes and pulled out an old golf ball. Did Jacob Kerr swing a club in his youth? Was it a pursuit put aside in his striving for a life of purity?

There was little superfluous in the life of Van Diemen's Land, he reflected. This was the home of an austere family who spent their days working and praying and attending church until, on the 14 June 1690, the place was visited by sudden frantic violence. The crime stood out starkly against the order he had found in every room. Was the motive simply to rob the house of a few bonds or notes? If that was so, it was an unsuccessful robbery. The killer had seemingly left little behind. No weapon, nothing dropped, only blood stains on the kitchen floor. To get the key, perhaps Kerr had to be killed. Perhaps there was something else in the kist that Mrs Kerr did not know about. Perhaps it caused Kerr's death. But why was the attack so savage? It hinted at delirium.

MacKenzie stood like a standing stone in a Highland field, deep in thought, until a sound outside roused him from his reverie. Yes, there was something else, he thought. Something was not quite right in the house. What he sensed in the house was not grief. Was it fear? Or was it rather what is left when fear has been vanquished?

He tried to open the small window in the north eaves but it was locked. He tried the larger window in the south eaves. It opened easily to reveal a ledge of about a foot and a half. He pushed up the sash window as high as it would go, letting fresh air flood the garret, carrying with it the sounds of the city, the noise of business and pleasure, a stark contrast to the silence of the house. There was little of the noise of life in Van Diemen's Land. The Tron Kirk Bell began to chime in the distance on the High Street. He waited to count 12.

The ledge was big enough to stand on if you were inclined. You could manoeuvre yourself out of the window relatively easily, if you had no fear of heights. It was difficult for a man of MacKenzie's size, he was well over six feet tall, but it would be easy for a smaller person like Scougall. He ducked his head and leaned out of the window, putting a foot onto the ledge, as the window was only a couple of feet above the floor, and looked down into the courtyard at the front of the house, holding onto the wall inside – a drop of perhaps 60 feet. He saw a stocky woman and a boy coming out the vennel and making their way across the courtyard towards the house. He surmised they were the cook Agnes and her son Thomas. Then a moment later something peculiar caught his attention.

Jane had just come out of Van Diemen's Land and was going in the opposite direction towards the wynd. She did not greet Agnes but hurried past as if in some kind of trance, ignoring the cook completely. He caught the withering look Agnes turned on her, a scathing look of disgust, even discernible from his position high above. He retreated back into the attic. There was something else he must consider – the relationship between the servants in the house. There were petty jealousies in every household. He remembered the fragment of fabric he had found in the range. He took it from his pocket. It was mostly burned, but it was still recognisable as a piece of cloth. How had it found its way into the range the night before? Was it just a piece of discarded rag or was it something else?

CHAPTER 4

The Household of Van Diemen's Land

MACKENZIE RETURNED TO the first floor and knocked on the living chamber door. Mrs Kerr was standing at the window again, gazing out. He coughed to get her attention. 'I've completed my examination of the house, madam. Could you summon your daughter? It's important I speak with everyone else now.'

She nodded expressionlessly and went to the fireplace where she rang a small bell on a table. When there was no answer after a couple of minutes, she smiled nervously. 'I'll fetch her, Mr MacKenzie.' Then turning, she continued, 'You must excuse me, sir. I forgot to check the plate and other valuables. I'm distracted in my thoughts. I will do that also.'

MacKenzie was left alone for a few minutes and took the opportunity to examine the room again. Another portrait of Kerr and his wife was on the wall facing the windows. Again, it revealed Kerr's considerable bulk, a dark serious face enclosed in a longer, fuller wig. His belt and pouch rested on a substantial paunch. There was the same arrogant look of self-assurance in his eyes. His obedient wife sat beside him with stern face. It was a singular portrait, painted, he judged, a few years after the one in the office downstairs. There were flecks of grey in Mrs Kerr's dark hair. They looked a grim, unhappy couple. MacKenzie read the signature at the bottom. Again the artist was Dutch.

A few minutes later, the door opened and Mary entered. She took the seat opposite MacKenzie with head bowed, not meeting his eyes. MacKenzie got a better look at her this time. She was thin to the point of emaciation and bore little resemblance to her mother. MacKenzie was reminded of a startled fawn and smiled sympathetically. 'I'm very sorry for your loss, Mary. It must be a grave shock to lose your father like this.'

She did not look up at him but nodded nervously. She was shaking, although the room was warm.

'Your mother will have told you why I'm here. It's due to the manner of your father's death. It was not a… natural death. It was a violent one. It was murder, my dear. We must find out what happened to him. The law demands it.'

He waited a moment to gauge her reaction. She nodded and held her tiny hands tightly together on her lap, but still did not meet his eyes. 'Just a few questions then you can go', he added, reassuringly.

Sensing her shyness, he proceeded gently with his questions. There was no need for any rough tactics yet. No need to apply any old lawyer's tricks. He made an effort to lighten his face, forcing himself to smile. 'Can you describe what happened this morning, Mary? Tell me as much as you can. Every detail is important.' He removed a notebook and pencil from his pocket to indicate he wanted her to talk.

She stared down at her hands as she spoke. 'I awoke at dawn as usual, sir. I got out of bed and looked out the window. I remember thinking it was a fine day. I was dressing when I heard screams downstairs. I met my mother in the hall. She must have heard the screams too. I followed her down to the kitchen. I remember her putting her arm out to stop me entering. But I saw everything anyway. He was lying in a pool of blood. I think I screamed. It was such a shock to see father there. Mother told me to go upstairs and wait in my room. I returned to my room and prayed for father's soul. I knew he was dead. Mother came up in a little while and told me he was taken by the Lord. We would never see him again... in this world. We might see him in the next world if we were all saved by the Lord at the end of time.'

MacKenzie waited again before asking another question, slightly surprised by the seemingly unemotional way she spoke about the events of the morning. She did not appear devastated by her father's death. She came across as nervous and agitated, but not distraught. However, each person responded differently to death, he thought. 'Who else was in the kitchen when you came downstairs, Mary?' he asked.

She thought for a moment before replying. 'Agnes was standing in front of my mother beside the table. I did not see Jane or Thomas.'

'Did you see a weapon anywhere?'

She was silent again before continuing in a monotone. 'I don't think so. I was only there for a moment. I could not stop looking at the blood.' The thought of this seemed to rouse her and her voice faltered, revealing the first hint of emotion. A tear appeared in the corner of her eye and ran down her pale, gaunt cheek.

'When was the last time you spoke to your father?' asked MacKenzie.

She closed her eyes to concentrate. 'Last night when he came to me... he came to my chamber to say good night about nine o'clock, after he had locked up the house. I was reading my Bible. He came into my chamber, as he always did, just to say good night and God rest my soul and kiss me goodnight.'

'There was no hint of anything different? Did he look troubled?' MacKenzie asked, looking up from his notebook, but she still did not raise her head to look at him directly.

She shook her head. 'He looked the same as usual. He was always the same. He was the same every day of his life, until I saw him lying on the kitchen floor this morning. Then I realised he was changed for good.'

MacKenzie thought it was a strange way to describe her father's death but continued with his questions. 'What about the house last night, Mary? Did you hear anything unusual during the night?'

She looked up at him timidly, gaining in confidence as she continued to speak, and meeting his eyes for the first time for a brief moment. 'I went straight to bed after praying, sir. I think mother was already in bed. Agnes and Jane and Thomas were in their rooms. I fell asleep soon after.'

'Did you hear anything during the night?' he asked again.

She thought for a moment. 'I was woken at some point. I don't know what time it was. It was still dark so it must have been before dawn. There was a sound somewhere in the house. At the time I thought someone had gone downstairs. It's not uncommon for mother to descend during the night, if she cannot sleep, or Jane to go down for a drink. Sometimes if I cannot sleep, I will go down to fetch a drink. And my father sometimes rose before dawn if he was preparing an order. Sometimes he did not sleep either. So, there were often noises in the house at night. It did not trouble me in the least. I fell asleep again.'

'What kind of sound was it, Mary?'

'Like something being dropped, something heavy falling on the floor, loud enough to wake me. Not the sound of a cat or dog or cry from a drunk on the street. It was not like that. It was not a sound from outside. I'm sure it was inside the house.'

'Could it have been the sound of a door being broken open?'

She nodded but said nothing more.

MacKenzie sighed. 'This is a more difficult question, my dear. I have to ask it because of the manner of your father's death.' He waited for her to meet his eyes again, which she did. 'Do you know of any reason why he might've been killed?'

She did not reply and her head dropped. She looked down at her hands. Her confidence had faded. She was trembling again, her tiny hands resting on her lap like a collection of bones. There were tears on her cheeks. 'I don't know, sir', she replied, her voice almost imperceptible.

'Did he have any enemies? Were there any men in the city who did not get on with him, Mary?'

'I cannot think of any, sir. Mother said it was a robbery.'

MacKenzie nodded thoughtfully. 'It might have been. We don't know for certain, yet.' He let his eyes wander round the room, before adding, 'How was everything in the house?'

She raised her head to look at him in the eyes once more. He noticed the skin of her face was pulled tightly over her cheekbones. She must hardly eat a morsel, he thought. 'What do you mean, sir?' she asked.

'How were relations between your mother and father?'

She appeared unsettled by the question. 'You cannot mean my mother would stab my father in the night?'

MacKenzie shook his head, maintaining a friendly demeanour. 'I'm not suggesting anything in particular, Mary. I just want to know if they were on good terms.'

'Yes. I believe they were, sir.'

'And what about relations between you and your father?'

Again, she did not reply immediately. She finally looked up at him and spoke in a hoarse whisper: 'I loved him, sir.'

'And the other servants? How did your father get on with Jane and Agnes and Thomas?' MacKenzie repeated the names methodically to fix them in his mind.

'He was a good master to them. This was a good house, sir. This was a house in which the precepts of the Lord were followed rigorously. It was called a holy house by the sisters. We did not deserve to be robbed. My father did not deserve to be slain in his own house. There are many sinners in this nation, sir. It is a sign of the times, surely, that a man is killed in his own house like this.' She shook her head before continuing to speak with more force, increasing the volume of her voice. 'Satan walks in this realm. Satan has walked in this house. Satan visited us last night. Satan slew my father!'

MacKenzie nodded affably but was thinking she appeared a troubled girl. 'How do you occupy yourself, Mary? You mentioned a sisterhood?'

She eyed him suspiciously. 'Like any daughter, I help my mother in the house. I serve the Lord and pray with my sisters. I am principally concerned with my immortal soul. I am concerned with the question of where my soul is bound at the end of time, as all God's creatures should be.'

It was a strange answer to make at such a time. But the Kerrs were a devout family. 'You referred to your sisters, Mary? I thought you an only child?' asked MacKenzie.

'I refer to my spiritual sisters, sir. My sisters in Christ. I belong to a sisterhood of true believers. We come together for prayer. We attend sermons throughout the land. My mother attends and Jane, as do many girls and women from the town. We are holy folk seeking a good life by serving the Lord.'

The city was full of sects, MacKenzie reflected, usually under the influence of some fanatic or other who claimed a vision of truth. Some had a political purpose, others were simply prayer groups. 'You'll be married someday, my dear?' he probed.

For the first time there was a flicker of a smile on the corner of her thin lips. 'I do not know. My father was waiting until I was older. I do not know what will happen now he's gone.'

'You may have a house of your own one day', MacKenzie said as he closed the notebook on his lap.

'I'm content here with my mother, sir. One day, perhaps. If it must be so, I will marry, if I have to.'

MacKenzie placed the pencil on top of the notebook. 'Thank you for answering my questions, Mary. I would like to speak to Agnes. Will you go and fetch her?'

He watched her leave the room, reminded of a stork with a voice. How she stood out in contrast to her father's corpulence.

Agnes entered the room a few minutes later, still wearing a kitchen apron over a dark dress. She had a ruddy complexion with curls of red hair poking out from her white cook's hat. She was stout with a thickset neck and looked disgruntled at being taken away from her work. She stood at the door, waiting to be asked to enter. 'Mary said you wanted to speak to me, sir.' There was a hint of irritation in her voice.

'Please have a seat, Agnes. Just a few questions', said MacKenzie, perfunctorily.

She limped over to the chair and sat down opposite him, looking uncomfortable.

MacKenzie continued affably, although he was finding it an increasing strain to maintain a smiling face. Something in the house was unsettling him. 'What do you think happened to your master, Agnes?'

'I hear a thief got in during the night and killed him, sir', she said bluntly as if describing what would be on the table for that night's dinner.

'Why do you say that?'

'My mistress says the back door was broken open and there is money missing from a kist.'

MacKenzie nodded. 'It's possible it was a botched robbery. We shall see.' He opened the notebook again and raised the pencil, before asking, 'How old are you, Agnes?'

She looked annoyed by the question. 'I'm 26 years, sir. What's that got to do with anything?'

MacKenzie ignored her petulance. 'How long have you served in the house?'

'Since I was a girl of 14. I've been here 12 years. Why do you need to know that?'

Again, MacKenzie ignored her and continued with his questions. 'That's a long time, Agnes. Has it been a good house to serve in?'

She eyed him suspiciously before answering, narrowing her eyes. 'It has, sir. It's a good, holy house. A house in which nothing much happened... until today.'

MacKenzie waited for a few moments, staring at her intently, then asked, 'You have a child, Agnes?'

'A boy called Thomas.'

'Are you married?' he asked, surmising she was not.

Again, she looked annoyed and shook her head. 'His father abandoned us without a word of farewell. Ran off to the Dutch army. I don't know if he's dead or alive. He's never seen the boy.'

MacKenzie shook his head and sought the pipe in his pocket. He held it for a few moments in his hand but did not take it out. 'A common tale, Agnes. I'm sorry for you.'

'I'm more fortunate than many, sir. I still have my bairn and we have a roof over our heads.'

'Did you have the child while you served in this house?' he asked.

She hesitated and looked away for a moment. 'I don't know what this has to do with the master's death, sir.'

'I want you to answer all my questions, Agnes.' MacKenzie kept his gaze firmly on her and his expression darkened.

She looked down at her hands, disarmed by the severity of his look, her confidence draining away. 'I did, sir. They showed me... they showed me Christian compassion. They did not cast me out on the street as some might have done. I had sinned. I was a fornicator. I attended the Session and confessed my sins. I sat on the stool before the congregation four Sabbaths running. I was humiliated before the parish. I felt their scorn. I was punished. It was just. I deserved it, sir. I had transgressed the Lord's precepts by letting filthy lust into my heart. I will never do it again. I will not give myself to any man, unless I am married to him. My bairn was delivered safely, thank God. I was allowed to bring him up in this house, helped by the mistress. I've much to thank the master and mistress for.'

'How old is your boy now?'

'Ten years old. The master was looking after his education. It was intended Thomas would be apprenticed with a merchant or writer, the master and mistress only having one child. Now I don't know what will happen to him.'

MacKenzie still fiddled with the empty pipe in his pocket. 'Tell me what happened this morning, Agnes.'

She took a deep breath and sighed. 'I'm always up before the dawn. I'm first up in the house, even before Jane. I wake up the rest of them. I knocked on all the doors as usual and went down to the kitchen to start preparing breakfast. It was like any other day. Little did I know what I was about to find.

'As soon as I entered, I saw him on the floor. I couldn't understand what had happened at first. I thought he had fallen over. He never drank much wine, so I dismissed the thought he was drunk. I saw blood and noticed he was lying in a strange way. It was then I realised he was dead. I remember the shock of it. Day after day it was the same routine, year after year the same. I enter the kitchen and check the range and begin my duties. And then today I find the master lying on his stomach with blood everywhere. I saw holes in his nightshirt and realised he'd been stabbed – many times.

I don't know how long I stood staring at him. I think I began to scream for help.

'Mrs Kerr appeared at my shoulder, perhaps a few minutes later. She almost fainted when she saw him. I had to hold her up on her feet. Then Mary was beside her, screaming madly. Mrs Kerr told her to go back to her room. When she was gone, my son appeared. I did not want him to see anything, so I took him upstairs myself before he had time to linger. I told him what had happened to the master when we were back in our chamber.'

'Did you see a weapon anywhere in the kitchen, Agnes?'

'No, sir. But one of my knives is missing. I noticed it right away. I keep them all on the work table by the sink.'

'Have you been back inside the kitchen?'

'Not since this morning, sir. I was waiting to be told I could get on with my work. I washed the stairs and the floor in the corridor as Mrs Kerr told me. There was an awful mess all the way to the front door caused by the guards lifting the master out the house.'

MacKenzie reflected for a moment. This must explain why there were only bloodstains on the kitchen floor. 'Can you think of any reason why Mr Kerr would be attacked, Agnes?'

She shook her head earnestly. 'He was a God-fearing man, sir. You'll see it from the painting there. He did all his business by the book. His word was his bond. He worshipped the Lord with vigour. He worked and prayed and served the Lord. That was his life, sir. That was all he ever did.'

'Do you attend the sisterhood with Mrs Kerr and her daughter?'

She shook her head, dismissively. 'I've no time for any sisterhood with all my duties in the house and a boy to take care of. I've no time to wander the fields or take the road to far off places like Dalkeith or Lasswade to hear ministers. I don't have the leisure for that, sir. Jane is lucky she's allowed to attend. She's only a servant like me, nothing more, although she thinks she's above me.'

MacKenzie recalled the withering look she had given Jane in the courtyard. 'What do they do in the sisterhood, Agnes?' he asked.

'They come together to pray. Helen Sim had a vision of an angel a few years ago. She's the relict of Robert Sim. The angel told her how she must serve the Lord. Others began to join her. When the sisters gather, they are seized by the Holy Spirit. They say they enter trances, although I've also heard some of them –' She suddenly stopped herself in mid-sentence and her face coloured.

'Some of them…?' MacKenzie repeated, looking up from his notebook.

'Some of them just like the look of the young ministers. I've heard them gossiping. How Mr Leitch has a handsome face. How Mr Innes would make a good husband. Is that serving the Lord, sir?'

MacKenzie ignored her question and continued. 'How many sisters are there?'

'Maybe 30 or 40 from the city and nearby villages. They are mostly wives of merchants and writers, their servants and maids. Helen Sim is the guiding light. She's a creature all right is Helen Sim. She's full of the Holy Spirit.'

'Where might I find her?'

'She bides in Tait's Land.'

After noting the address, MacKenzie's face lightened. 'Is this a happy house, Agnes?' he asked, nonchalantly.

She looked surprised by the question and did not answer immediately but fidgeted with the hem of her apron and eyed him sourly. Finally, after an uncomfortable minute's silence she answered. 'I would not describe it as that, sir. It is a… it is a serious house. Yes, I would call it a serious house.

Mr Kerr was serious in all he did. He was serious in business and serious in religion. It was no place of jollity. It was a place where…' Again, she trailed off, not completing what she was about to say.

'A place where…?' repeated MacKenzie.

'A place where… the Lord was served', she said firmly. MacKenzie was sure she was going to say something else. He waited but she did not say anything more.

'What about relations in the family, Agnes, relations between Mr Kerr and his wife and daughter?'

She did not answer, hesitating again. But this time it was as if she was choosing her words carefully. 'A devoted husband and father, sir.'

'How did he treat you and your son?'

Again, she paused momentarily. 'He was a strict master. I will say that. He was strict with Thomas but he was little trouble if you followed his orders. I kept a clean and regular house and cooked him a good dinner. There may be more lenient masters in this city, but there are also crueller ones.'

'How did he treat Jane?'

The mention of her name seemed to touch a raw nerve and Agnes' expression changed. The thought of the younger maid clearly got under her skin. MacKenzie wondered if it was just a rivalry common amongst servants or something deeper. 'You'll have to ask her… she's… she's a bit above herself, that girl!' she exclaimed.

'What do you mean, Agnes?'

'She's had some schooling. I've had none. I've had a harder life than her. I'm an orphan, sir. She looks down on me. She thinks she's above me because she can read and write and… and because she attends the sisterhood with the mistress and Mary. She's closer in age to Mary than I am and they are thick together. We should not be so arrogant to imagine we are better than each other. We are all the same in God's eyes.'

MacKenzie nodded in agreement. 'I've one last question for now, Agnes', he said, closing the notebook. 'Have you seen anyone hanging around the courtyard or vennel recently? Has anyone been watching the house? A thief often makes plans before committing a crime.'

'No, sir. I've seen nothing unusual.'

MacKenzie indicated with a friendly gesture of his hand the interview was over. 'Thank you, Agnes. If you could find Jane, I want to question her now.'

As Agnes rose to leave, she lowered her voice and whispered to him, looking apprehensive. 'Should I be concerned about the safety of my son in this house, sir?'

MacKenzie replied reassuringly. 'Don't worry, Agnes. We'll get to the bottom of it. Just keep your door locked at night as a precaution.'

Jane entered a few minutes later and took the same seat opposite him. He did not question her immediately but observed her carefully as she sat before him. She was pretty in an unusual way with dark complexion and slightly bulging eyes, reminding him of the women he had courted in Italy during his travels as a young man. She appeared less nervous than the other members of the household.

'How long have you worked here, Jane?' he asked.

'Not long, sir. About a year or so.' MacKenzie reflected she appeared untroubled by the killing. Perhaps it was because she was not related to the deceased and had not lived in the house long.

'How did you get the position here?'

'I met Mary at the sisterhood. My mother knows Mistress Sim. We prayed together in the fields many times before I came here. Mrs Kerr asked me if I would come to serve them once she knew me better, once she knew I was devout in the service of the Lord.' She spoke fluently and confidently for a servant, reflected MacKenzie.

'How have you found your time here?' he asked.

'I like it, sir. I have my own room on the third floor. I do not have to share as I did at home. I love having my privacy. It allows me to serve the Lord.'

'How old are you?'

'Seventeen years, sir.'

MacKenzie's face darkened and he moved forward in his chair to stare at her intently. 'Tell me what happened this morning, Jane.'

She continued to speak calmly, seemingly unperturbed by his attempt to unsettle her. 'I was woken by Agnes as usual. She knocks on my door at six every morning. I got out of bed and got down on my knees to pray. I prayed to the Lord for a few minutes. I was dressing when I heard screams downstairs. I went straight down to the kitchen where I found a commotion. Agnes and Mrs Kerr were there and Mary was leaving in tears. She passed me without saying a word. When I looked into the kitchen, I saw the master lying on the floor. At first, I thought he had fallen down and wondered why no one helped him up. But Mrs Kerr was saying again and again he was slain. I noticed blood on the floor and observed wounds on his back. I realised he had been killed. Then Thomas appeared and Agnes took him away before he saw anything. I stood with Mrs Kerr looking down on him. It was an awful sight. Agnes returned a few minutes later and told me to run to the Tolbooth to fetch the Guard.'

MacKenzie was impressed by the composed, observant way she described the events of the morning. 'What about last night, Jane?'

'What do you mean, sir?'

'Tell me what you did last night. Tell me everything you can remember happening in the house.'

She looked unsettled for a moment but regained her composure. 'I retired to my chamber early to pray. I prayed for an hour. I read my Bible. I read a couple of Rutherford's letters. I always find them instructive. I heard the master locking up with Thomas. They always do it at the same time. I went to bed and fell asleep. I did not wake until the morning.'

'Did you hear anything during the night?'

'No, sir.'

'Mary says she heard a noise.'

'I heard it not, sir. But it's often noisy on the High Street with drunken screams and shouts almost every night. I've grown used to it. I sleep soundly, especially if I have found the Lord in prayer before my slumber. Then I sleep with contentment. It takes a hard knock to wake me in the morning. Agnes will tell you. A few times she's been unable to rouse me and I've been scolded by her.'

'Can you think of anyone who would want to harm Mr Kerr?'

'Agnes said it was a robbery.'

'Why would a thief kill your master so savagely?'

She shook her head. 'I know not why, sir. He was a pious man. He was an elder in the Session. He gave much money to charity. He was hard-working and devout in the service of the Lord. He will surely be in Heaven. He will surely be with the Lord, will he not sir?' she said, almost smiling at him, before looking down at her hands.

'I know nothing of such matters, my dear', MacKenzie replied, sharply. He wondered how on earth a man like Kerr could be counted among the Elect, if there was such a thing. 'Now, tell me about the sisterhood you belong to?'

She smiled, seemingly pleased to talk about something else. 'We are just a prayer group, sir, started by Helen Sim, a worthy woman. We pray in the open air around the town and in the rigs beyond the city. Sometimes we travel to hear preachers, as far away as Lasswade. I've even travelled across the firth to Largo. We like to question the ministers about their sermons. We fight sin with prayer, sir. We fight blasphemy with prayer. We fight the blasphemy infecting this land with prayer. Satan walks among us, sir. He's always at our side. We must fight him with prayer.' She stopped for a moment before adding conspiratorially, 'I've seen him, sir.'

MacKenzie raised his eyebrows. 'Who have you seen, Jane?'

'Satan, sir. I've seen him. I've seen the Devil... here.' She placed a finger on her temples. 'When I dream at night, I see him. Also, I've seen him watching us when we pray in the fields.'

MacKenzie was surprised by her talk of Satan, especially as she continued to speak without any emotion in her voice in such a matter of fact way, as if it was the most natural thing in the world.

'What does he look like, Jane?' he asked.

'He's a dark handsome man, sir. He wears a long black cloak and black breeches and long leather boots. He aims to trap us. He aims to take us as his own. We must always be on our guard for Satan, sir. But do not worry. We can fight him with prayer.'

MacKenzie nodded, but a feeling of despair passed through him. Under his breath he cursed the ministry who filled young heads with such nonsense. 'Agnes does not attend the sisterhood?' he asked.

'I believe she has... she has... she has sinned in the past... she is not ready to be accepted among us. She has not shown true contrition.' A hint of smugness was evident in her reply.

'She has sinned?' asked MacKenzie.

'It's well known, sir. She's guilty of fornication. She fell with child many years ago. She fornicated with a soldier out of wedlock. She had to sit on the stool of repentance in the Kirk. I believe she's still tainted by that sin. The sisterhood are pure of heart. Many of us are assured of God's grace despite our young age. I fear Agnes is still polluted by lust. She looks not on us with a warm heart. But she may repent one day. She may, one day, join us in the worship of the Lord.'

'How did Mr Kerr treat his servants?' asked MacKenzie, changing the subject abruptly.

'He was always respectful to me, although strict.'

'Did he ever raise his hand to you, Jane?'

She shook her head. 'He had no reason to. I'm devoted to my work. I performed all the duties he requested of me. I gave him no trouble, sir. I gave him no reason to strike me.'

'What about Agnes and the boy?'

'I know not about Agnes. The boy is sometimes absent minded. He wanders off and forgets himself. He forgets the messages he's sent for. When he behaved badly, he was beaten by the master, but not severely. I believe he deserved the punishment, sir.'

'How did your master treat his wife and daughter?'

'As a father and husband should, I believe.'

MacKenzie thought he was making little progress with the interrogation. 'Is there anything else you can tell me about your master's death, Jane?'

She shook her head.

MacKenzie smiled at her, making an effort to lighten his expression. 'Tell Agnes I'll speak with Thomas now.'

The Tron Kirk bell sounded once as he waited. His stomach was telling him it was time to eat, but it would have to wait. Thomas entered reluctantly with his mother. He was a serious-looking red-haired boy with a narrow face and darting eyes, dressed in brown breeches and a jacket which was slightly too tight.

'Sit down', MacKenzie said gently. Agnes stood beside her son, resting a hand on his shoulder.

MacKenzie smiled at the boy. 'I have a few questions, Thomas. I'll be done soon.'

Thomas nodded nervously. He held his hands together in front of him, as if being questioned at school by the dominee.

'Last night you passed through the house with your master locking up as usual', stated MacKenzie.

Thomas nodded.

'Could you tell me exactly what you did with him?'

There was silence for a few seconds until Agnes nudged her son, encouraging him to speak. 'I always walked a few paces behind him, sir', said Thomas. 'It was the same every night. The master demanded I did not speak while we locked up. First, we locked the back door on the ground floor. Then the front door with another key. Then we closed the windows on the ground floor and made sure they were secure. Then we checked the kitchen in the basement. Then the windows on the first floor. I put out all the candles in the kitchen, hall and living chamber. Then I went to bed.'

'Was there anything different about last night?' asked MacKenzie.

'It was the same every night. I've done it for as long as I can remember. That's the way the master liked it. He liked everything in order. He liked everything in the right place. Nothing was ever out of place.'

'Was your master in a good mood last night, Thomas?'

The boy stopped himself for a moment. 'No. I would not say he was in a good mood, sir.' He turned to give his mother a nervous look before continuing. 'He was not in a bad mood either. He was the same as he ever was.'

'Did he say anything to you as you passed round the house?'

'Not a word. He never spoke a word. He demanded complete silence when we locked up. He was listening for anything outside the house.'

'Was he worried about being robbed?'

The boy nodded.

'After you went to bed did you hear anything in the night?'

'Nothing, sir.'

'Where do you sleep, Thomas?'

'With my mother, sir. On the third floor.'

MacKenzie continued to question him affably. 'You've answered my questions very well, Thomas. I've just a few more, then you can run off and play.' The boy relaxed and the strained expression on his face was replaced with a flicker of a smile.

'Did you like your master, Thomas?' MacKenzie asked.

The smile disappeared and he stole another look at his mother. MacKenzie noticed her hand, resting on his shoulder, was shaking slightly. 'Of course, sir. He was the master', replied the boy.

'So, you're sorry he's dead, Thomas?' MacKenzie did not like putting pressure on such a young child but sometimes it was necessary.

The boy looked confused and turned to his mother again. She encouraged him to answer. 'I'm not too sorry, sir', he said. 'The master is now in Heaven where we all desire to go, some day. The master was bound there as a righteous man. He was an elder and a man of the Session. He will be rewarded for his devotion during this life.' Thomas spoke as if he had rehearsed his reply.

MacKenzie smiled at the thought. Elders were usually trouble in his book. He hated the self-righteousness of those who placed themselves between ordinary folk and their supposed maker. In his experience, they were often charlatans. 'You're right, Thomas. If he's in Heaven why should we be sorry about it? He has escaped this world of pain. But it's not always the case that elders are good men. Why do you think he's in Heaven?'

Again, the boy looked puzzled by the question. 'He told me himself, sir. He told me he had assurance from God. He told me God had spoken to him many times when he prayed. He was told he was one of those chosen by the Lord. His soul was saved from the start of time. He told me if I wanted to be saved like him, if I wanted to avoid the agony of damnation, I should live an obedient life. I should always do as I was told. I should always respect and obey him.'

'And did you?' asked MacKenzie, a hint of a smile on his face.

Thomas nodded seriously. 'I did, sir.'

'How do you get on with your mistress and her daughter Mary?'

Thomas looked uncomfortable again and began to fidget. His mother finally butted in. 'I don't think he understands you, sir. They are part of his family. He's always lived in this house. He knows nothing else.'

MacKenzie turned to the boy again, encouragingly, and waited for a reply.

'They are good to us', Thomas said finally, turning back to his mother who gave him a strained smile.

'What about Jane?' asked MacKenzie.

'I like her', Thomas said without hesitation. 'She's teaching me to read and write.'

MacKenzie turned to Agnes and caught a hint of a frown on her face.

'How do you progress in your studies, Thomas?' he asked.

'Well, sir.'

MacKenzie rose to stretch his back and stood for a few moments looking down on the boy. He reflected that Van Diemen's Land was an austere environment to be brought up in, so different from his own carefree upbringing in the Highlands. There was something sombre about all the inhabitants of Van Diemen's Land. There was a joylessness about the household which he found disturbing. He walked over to Thomas and tapped his shoulder with an avuncular hand. 'Thank you both for now.'

MacKenzie waited for them to leave the room, then went downstairs. He found Mrs Kerr in the business premises on the ground floor, checking through the stock of cloth. He told her he was leaving for now, and she could have the kitchen floor cleaned. He would see himself out.

CHAPTER 5

Investigations in Cumming's Court

MACKENZIE CLOSED THE front door carefully and stepped out into Cumming's Court, the courtyard in front of the house. Although it was early in the afternoon, the courtyard was already cast in shadow by the high buildings. He heard footsteps and voices. A few people appeared from Cockburn's Wynd, just folk going about their daily business; a messenger on an errand; a clerk almost running, late for a meeting; a laird and lady sauntering leisurely who nodded at him in recognition – Sir John Swinton of that Ilk and his wife; and two ministers shuffling in black robes, like a couple of ancient ravens.

The General Assembly of the Kirk was due to meet for the first time in decades and many old ministers, the so-called antediluvians, had come to Edinburgh to oversee the demise of the bishops. He wondered what the momentous change would mean for Scotland after 30 years of episcopacy. The bishops had not brought peace to church or country, but neither had presbytery brought peace before that. When you thought about it, there had been little harmony in Scotland since the Reformation of 1560. That event had fractured the old church and kindled unrest in the hearts of the people. During the Covenanting years, the nation was ruled by a fanatical faction. Scotland was always divided about something. Now King William wanted to quell dissent north of the border and crush the Jacobites in Ireland. There was much at stake.

The new King had not visited Scotland and apparently had no intention of doing so. That was a grave error. Another Gaelic saying came to MacKenzie. They were coming thick and fast today. A kingdom without a king is like a snail without a shell. He chuckled to himself. There was more wisdom in the aphorisms of his people than in the works of all the philosophers in his library at the Hawthorns. He shook his head and turned his attention to the other tenements.

He walked up to the door of the house on the left of Van Diemen's Land. It was its mirror image, built around the same time and attached to it, although the door was dark green rather than black. 'Henderson's Land' was carved on the lintel. The door was answered by a young servant girl.

'May I speak with your master?' MacKenzie asked, after introducing himself.

She went back inside and returned a minute later to let him in. Following her up the stairs to the first floor, he was shown into a sitting room where an old couple sat before a fire. They both looked pleased to see him and smiled warmly. Their days were no doubt quiet with little incident. They would enjoy a visit from a stranger.

MacKenzie introduced himself and the old man, wearing a red dressing gown, rose to shake his hand, but his wife, who wore a mauve one, remained in her chair, indicating she had trouble getting to her feet.

'I'm John Douglas, sir. My wife, Janet. It's a pleasure to meet you. I worked as a secretary for the Earl of Linlithgow. I'm now retired. We get few visitors these days. Most of our friends and relations are departed from this world. You say you were Clerk of the Session. I think I remember you, Mr MacKenzie.'

'I lost my position at the revolution', said MacKezie. 'A glorious revolution they are calling it!'

Douglas eyed him carefully then chuckled. 'I see you are a sceptic like me. A glorious revolution indeed! Folk getting hot about everything; marching up and down the High Street, attacking respectable people in their homes. A terrible business is revolution.' He waited for a moment to gauge MacKenzie's reaction. When he saw him smiling gently, he continued. 'Good for nobody. I should know. I've seen enough of them. They always start with good intentions. I was a young man when they signed the Covenant in Greyfriar's Kirkyard. All the great men signed it, including Montrose. But a few years later Montrose was trying to kill those who stood beside him that day.' Douglas shook his head and was lost in the past for a few moments before continuing. 'I was dumbstruck when they killed King Charles. How could they do such a thing? How could they think that killing a king would solve anything? I will never forget the day. My mother fainted when she heard the news. We thought she had dropped dead. Is there any greater sin than killing your king? Then there was rejoicing when his son was restored. But rebellion after rebellion followed. And now the other son is forced to flee and the crown taken by his own daughter who is married to a Dutchman! Young fools will always be attracted to revolution. It will be different this time, they say. The changes are necessary for the common good. But the rich get richer and the poor stay poor, whatever happens.' Douglas smiled again.

Despite his pessimistic interpretation of Scottish history, Douglas looked remarkably optimistic for an old man near the end of his days, MacKenzie reflected. He nodded in agreement with him and took the chair offered to him. 'The matter at hand, Mr Douglas. I'm appointed by the Advocate to investigate a case of murder. Have you heard what happened next door?'

'Yes. An awful business. Poor Mrs Kerr. A nice, quiet woman', replied Douglas.

'I have to ask some questions. You are the family's closest neighbours. How long have you lived here?'

'Not long, sir. About four years only. We took the place from my brother when he died.'

'So, you've known the family in Van Diemen's Land since then. How have you found them?'

The old man thought for a moment. 'I've found them well enough, although we have little to do with them. They are quiet, religious folk who keep themselves to themselves. Mrs Kerr is friendly but she's always rushing off somewhere when you meet her on the street. I'm sorry to say, for I do not like speaking ill of the dead, I found Kerr a cold fish. He was on the Kirk Session, you know. That made him feared by some. He would never stop long to chat. He never visited us once in four years, despite being invited many times. That's good neighbourliness for you; that's how the godly treat an old couple left with no family. He would say a word or two and be on his way. We are too old to go to the Kirk on the Sabbath. At least there are some benefits of old age!' Douglas chuckled.

MacKenzie could not help laughing with him. 'What about their daughter, Mr Douglas?' he asked.

'The girl's a frightened rabbit. I've never seen such a timid creature. She walks around with her head down in her mother's tail.' Douglas shook his head. 'It's appalling what's happened. We are told money is behind it. A thief broke in during the night. Money is behind most bad things on this earth, Mr MacKenzie. I dearly hope there's no need for filthy lucre in the next world', he smiled sardonically.

MacKenzie turned to Mrs Douglas, a tiny shrivelled woman who was nodding at everything her husband said. 'How did you find them, madam?'

She showed no sign of comprehension. 'My wife is deaf, sir', said Douglas. 'She does not go out much. How do you find them, my dear?' He moved forward in his chair and shouted in his wife's ear. She seemed to understand for she nodded and began to speak. 'A quiet family, sir. No trouble to us... a quiet, godly family. No trouble to us, sir. It's a terrible business when a man is slain in his own home, a terrible business.'

'Did you hear anything last night?' MacKenzie addressed the question to Mr Douglas.

'Nothing, Mr MacKenzie. I heard nothing last night.'

'Has anything unusual happened in the courtyard recently?'

Douglas thought for a moment but shook his head.

'Then I will not keep you any longer. Good day to you both. If you think of anything else, ask for me in Libberton's Wynd.'

'Will you not stay for a glass of wine, Mr MacKenzie?' asked Douglas. They both looked disappointed when he declined. MacKenzie would have liked to stay longer and share stories, in particular Douglas' recollections about Montrose. Perhaps he would pay them a visit when the case was solved.

Just as MacKenzie put his hand on the door handle, Douglas spoke again. 'I've just remembered one other thing, Mr MacKenzie. It may be nothing but it has stuck in my mind for some reason.'

MacKenzie turned and stood at the door. 'Go on, Mr Douglas.'

'A couple of weeks ago I was out in the courtyard. It was a pleasant day and I was taking a short walk. A man approached Van Diemen's Land and knocked loudly on the door. I was taken aback by the force with which he struck the door. It was not the maid who answered but Kerr himself. He ushered the man quickly inside.'

MacKenzie moved back into the room. 'Did you know the man?'

Douglas thought for a moment. 'I recognised him. But I cannot remember where I've come across him.'

'Could you describe him?' asked MacKenzie.

'He was dressed much like the next man. He wore black breeches, a dark cloak and a periwig. I got a look at his face for a moment. He had a large nose and ruddy complexion. I wish I could remember more about him. I know I've seen him somewhere.'

'Contact me if you remember, Mr Douglas. It could be important.'

'I've seen many men go in and out of Van Diemen's Land, sir. No doubt connected with Kerr's trade. But there was something about the way this fellow was knocking. That's why I remember it.'

The maid was waiting for MacKenzie outside in the hall. She stood nervously by the front door, looking like she had something to say but lacking the courage to say it. MacKenzie nodded towards the door in a friendly manner. She looked up at him fearfully. 'Is there something you want to say to me, my dear?' he asked.

She nodded and looked down at her feet. 'I must tell you something, sir', she whispered. 'It's about the Kerrs. I overheard you asking about them. My master and mistress are old. They do not see or hear much and their chamber is on the other side of the house. I sleep on the top floor on this side of the building.' She placed her hand on the wall joining Van Diemen's Land. 'I've not been here long, only a year. During that time, I've heard things, sir. I've heard horrible things at night!' Her expression was distressed.

'What things?' MacKenzie asked intensely.

She paused for a moment, gathering herself to continue. 'Awful things. Terrible screams and cries... I don't know how to describe them... as if someone was being put to the screws.'

'Was someone having nightmares?' asked MacKenzie.

She shook her head. 'I don't think so, sir. I thought the cries came from... different voices.'

'You mean more than one person was screaming?'

She nodded. 'I think so, at different times. I think I heard different voices.'

'How often have you heard such screams?'

'Once or twice a month. I'm woken up by them. The first time I was terrified. I must admit I'm looking for a position in another household. I want to get away from here.'

'Would you say a man or a woman was screaming?' asked MacKenzie.

'A woman, or maybe a girl. Or perhaps a young boy. I'm not talking about a cry or scream, like someone waking from a bad dream. It's something different. Something awful. Sometimes like the whimpers of an animal, other times howls of pain as if someone was being tortured. I cannot find any sleep after I've heard it.'

'Have you told anyone about what you've heard?'

She shook her head.

'Did you hear anything last night?'

She shook her head again. 'Nothing, sir. I've heard nothing for a week or so.'

'Can you remember the last time you heard something?'

She thought for a moment. 'I know exactly, sir. It was the Sabbath before last.'

'What's your name, my dear?'

'Alice Neil, sir.'

'How did you find Mr Kerr, Alice?'

She shook her head again. 'I did not like him, sir. I found him gruff. I did not like the way he looked at me. It made me feel dirty. He eyed me all over, like when you go into a tavern full of men who've been drinking, which I rarely do. He said nothing to me. He just looked at me.'

'What about Mrs Kerr?'

'She's pleasant enough but always eager to get away. She would never stop to talk. The daughter is a timid creature. She says nothing and barely raises her head. I would say she's terrified of something. I think they're both scared of him. They *were* both scared of him. That's the impression I got of them.'

MacKenzie nodded. 'Do you know the maid Jane and the cook Agnes and her son?'

'I know the maid a little. She's friendly but only talks about ministers and sermons and journeys to such and such Kirk to hear a sermon and how this minister preaches braw and another is a dullard. Agnes is always in a rush to be back indoors. She looks disgruntled all the time. The bairn is like any other child, sometimes happy as a lark, other times silent and sullen. I see him out and about on errands.'

'Thank you for telling me all this, Alice. Does anyone else live here with you?'

'No, sir.'

'What about the tenement over there?' MacKenzie pointed in the direction of the building on the east side of the courtyard.

'It's empty but should be rented by a new tenant soon.'

'Who owns it?'

'It belongs to Mrs Hair. But she doesn't live there. She rents it out for income.'

Mrs Hair's influence spread far and wide, MacKenzie thought. He left Alice and went to Learmonth's Land, the tenement on the west side of the courtyard, a building different in design from Van Diemen's Land, which had been constructed in the last 30 years. He knocked on the door but no one answered. He knocked again and waited for a couple of minutes. There was still no answer. He turned his back on the door and stood, staring back at Van Diemen's Land.

The impression of an out-of-the-way corner of the city came back to him, a place beyond the city's bustle, a place forgotten.

He went to the sandstone wall along the south side of the courtyard. It was over six feet high, so he could not see into the gardens on the other side. The back of the tenements on the High Street were a considerable distance from the courtyard. It would be a laborious task to ask all the inhabitants of these buildings if they had seen anything. He thought he had enough to be getting on with. It was a task he might have given Davie Scougall if he wasn't so busy working for Mrs Hair.

Scougall was waiting for him at their usual table at the back of the Periwig. He had abandoned the wig he wore in the office and his dark hair was held up in a ponytail. He had little interest in the case and was busy at work, but he found it difficult to say no to meeting MacKenzie. Scougall found it difficult to say no to anyone. 'I can only stay for one glass, sir. I must get home to Chrissie', he said anxiously as soon as MacKenzie took off his hat, called for some wine and stretched out beside him.

MacKenzie smiled. 'I'd forgotten you have a wife to be getting back to, Davie, and you're not at my beck and call', he jested. 'I won't keep you long. Just long enough to ask a favour or two. But first, what's the news in town?'

Scougall sipped his glass of claret, unnerved by the mention of favours, which usually involved being put out, and looked at the news sheet lying on the table which he had already perused. 'Parliament continues with its business, sir. The Act restoring presbytery will be passed soon. There's also news from Ireland. King William has landed with his army. It's thought he will face the old King in battle in a matter of weeks. And there's a consignment of oranges arrived from Amsterdam.'

MacKenzie lit his pipe and began to puff away contentedly, deep in thought. 'You'll soon have your beloved presbytery, Davie', he finally mused. 'But will the Scots be any happier with it? They're a thrawn lot. The days of the Covenant were hardly ones of peace and contentment. Remember the civil wars began up here, not in England, Davie. But you know your history.

'Before I forget', continued MacKenzie, taking a glass of wine from the waiter. 'I've started reading Archibald's book about the troubles. I would describe it as an instructive, if long-winded, account of the 1630s, detailing the causes of unhappiness which led to the Covenant. It will require some editing before publication. I may get you to check the proofs. We should get it to a printer soon.' MacKenzie reflected sadly that his dead friend had not visited him from beyond the grave to describe the nature of the afterlife as they had joked the first to die would do. Stirling did often appear in his dreams, however, and would share his thoughts with him. As a devout Jacobite, Stirling was naturally disgusted by recent political developments. He would have strong words against the restoration of presbytery.

Scougall did not feel like arguing about politics. He disagreed with MacKenzie on the matter of Bishop and presbytery and besides he was keen to get home to Chrissie and her delicious cooking. He was not used to having a person pleased to see him at the end of the day and he loved to hear the news she had heard in the markets and on the street. She knew more about what was going on in Edinburgh than him. It was lighter stuff than the murder of a merchant. He wondered if he had lost his appetite for helping MacKenzie with criminal cases. He had been excited by it when he was younger but he had better things to be getting on with now. 'How did you get on in Van Diemen's Land, sir?' he asked with little enthusiasm, just trying not to be rude.

MacKenzie took the pipe from his mouth and shifted forward in his seat, dropping his voice to a whisper so none of the other drinkers could hear. 'Let me tell you, Davie. I made a thorough examination of the building and questioned the five living inhabitants and an old couple and their servant next door. The facts I've established are these: Kerr was stabbed in the back 20 times sometime during the night and was found in the kitchen not long after dawn by Agnes the cook. A door on the ground floor was broken open during the night. Money or documents were taken from a kist in Kerr's office on the ground floor.'

'Then it was a disrupted robbery, sir', proposed Scougall, keen to see the thing over and done with.

MacKenzie nodded, but his expression told Scougall it was not that simple. 'That may be the case, Davie. But something unsettles me about that house. Something about the atmosphere is not quite right. The inhabitants are in a kind of mourning, but not conventional mourning. More like a stupor, or as if they have just woken from a stupor. I don't think they are in mourning for Kerr. My impression of him is unfavourable. He was a dark presence. Besides, the maid in the tenement next door has heard awful screams in Van Diemen's Land on a number of nights.'

Scougall put his glass down, becoming more interested. 'A member of the household is unhappy. That's not uncommon. Young women are prone to nightmares. My own twin sisters have been known to wail during the night, especially after bad dreams.'

'You're right, Davie. The atmosphere might be unrelated to the killing of Kerr. But sometimes you just get a feeling. Now to the favours I require of you.'

At the mention of this, Scougall looked eager to be off. He quickly finished his glass and took hold of his hat. 'I don't have much time at the moment, sir. The office is very busy.'

MacKenzie placed his hand on the hat, preventing Scougall from taking it. 'It will not take long and you will be helping me, Davie. I want you to ask your acquaintances who tend towards presbytery about Kerr and his family. Presbyterians will speak to you but they would say nothing to me as a despised Episcopalian. Learn as much as you can about the Kerr family. Tomorrow I'll speak with the minister about Kerr's work on the Session and Helen Sim about the sisterhood attended by the women in Van Diemen's Land. Do you know anything about such associations?'

Scougall let his hat rest on the table and sat back in resignation. 'They had their origins in the conventicles that met in the countryside before the revolution. They are usually groups of women who gather to pray and discuss religion... and politics.'

MacKenzie finished his glass in a gulp and called for another bottle. 'Enthusiasm in religion is a dangerous thing, Davie. Enthusiasm in most things spells trouble.'

Scougall reflected that he felt less enthusiastic about religion than he was in the past, recalling the hours he spent in prayer and reflection in his youth. His devotion was now limited to a brief prayer before getting into bed. He was now much more enthusiastic for the company of Chrissie. But he could not help saying to MacKenzie, 'You are an enthusiast too, sir. You are enthusiastic about your books. You always talk enthusiastically of Cicero and your garden and the game of golf. I am enthusiastic for Chrissie. I am also enthusiastic for golf and religion, which I know you do not share. We are both enthusiastic creatures, sir. All people are enthusiastic about something.' He had not meant to be so demonstrative, but he felt glad he was. It was the truth as he saw it.

MacKenzie smiled and sat back. 'You're getting wise in your old age, Davie Scougall. Perhaps enthusiastic is the wrong word. How about fanatical; being fanatical always results in trouble.'

'Are you not fanatical about the truth, sir?' Scougall's confidence was growing.

MacKenzie nodded again and took up his pipe. 'Perhaps I am, Davie.'

'The Presbyterians have a different kind of truth, sir. It's impossible to believe in someone else's truth', replied Scougall.

'You're right, Davie', said MacKenzie, filling his glass from the bottle placed on the table by the waiter. 'But these are troubling times. The ministers whip up people with talk of blasphemy and witches. They'll be burning old women again on the Castle Hill before we know it. Innocent men and women sacrificed for what? It's that kind of zealotry I despise.'

'I believe most Scots will be happier when presbytery is restored to the Kirk', mused Scougall, finding himself sipping from the glass MacKenzie had filled with claret.

'Half of Scots, perhaps, at most, Davie. What of the other half who have no liking for presbytery and Kirk Sessions? What does King William really want of Scotland? Does he care anything for the country? We have a King who has never set foot in the land he rules. And what will happen to that other King, the one in exile? Remember him, Davie? James Stuart, the man born of the loins of King Charles, who was the son of James Stuart, our own King James VI!'

MacKenzie took the bottle to pour another glass, but this time Scougall was adamant, placing his hand over it. 'I'm sorry, sir. I would love to stay and talk. I can see you're keen. I'm pleased to see you so animated. But Chrissie will be worried if I'm not back soon. I'll ask about Kerr tomorrow.'

MacKenzie smiled, filling his own glass to the brim with the ruby liquid, taking a mouthful and savouring it. 'Just one final thing, Davie.' He put his hand in his pocket and took out the piece of material he had found in the range. 'Ask Chrissie what she thinks of this. I found it in the kitchen of Van Diemen's Land. What is the cloth and what kind of garment has it come from?' Scougall took it and nodded. 'I'll have to drink all this myself', MacKenzie slurred. 'Enjoy your chicken fricassee!' He raised the glass and said something in Gaelic that Scougall did not understand. It was a toast to the King over the Water, James Stuart.

MacKenzie sat contentedly for another hour after Scougall left, smoking pipe after pipe and finishing the bottle, and another, while he ruminated on the case. The wine had a beneficial effect on him, allowing him to return to Van Diemen's Land in his mind and wander from room to room, recalling the conversations of earlier in the day. He placed the candle on the table in front of him and removed the rag from his other pocket to examine the specimens of hair from the kitchen. He held a single hair up to the candle. It was light in colour. It had not come from the head of Agnes, Thomas or Mrs Kerr. He turned to the bloody clump. It looked like tiny bits of skin were attached to the end of the hairs as if they had been yanked out of the scalp.

Once he had finished the bottle, he was convinced of a couple of things. Firstly, he hated the prospect of a Dutchman as King of Scots with all his heart. He would do all he could, within reason, to aid the return of King James. Secondly, he did not believe the killing in Van Diemen's Land was a botched robbery.

Later, he meandered down the High Street to his apartments in Libberton's Wynd in a state of inebriation, staggering once or twice, as he had drunk most of three bottles of wine. He stopped in a dark corner just off the High Street to relieve himself and, as he watched the stream of urine make its way towards the Cowgate, recalled the image that had come to him earlier in the day of Jacob Kerr perched on his chamber pot. He also remembered the spilt urine on the floorboards beside it. The mess stood out starkly against the cleanliness everywhere else in Van Diemen's Land.

When he had returned home, his old servant Archie helped him undress and get into bed. As his head hit the soft pillow, MacKenzie reflected that he was enjoying himself. He had not suffered a melancholic thought all day long. The black bird, his companion of many years, was not even a speck on the horizon of his mind. Investigating a murder was good for his soul.

CHAPTER 6

A Visit to St Giles Kirk

ARCHIE INTERRUPTED BREAKFAST the next morning to deliver a letter from MacKenzie's daughter, Elizabeth. She begged him to be careful and return to the Hawthorns as soon as possible. Geordie was missing him. MacKenzie wrote a short reply, reassuring her he would be back as soon as the case was solved. It would only be a matter of days. He left his apartments and headed for St Giles Kirk, a few minutes' walk away.

He found the atmosphere in St Giles oppressive and the silence spoke to him of the joyless message of Scottish Protestantism. He shook his head at the stools of repentance where sinners were humiliated for transgressions from blasphemy to fornication, and the long, uncomfortable pews where parishioners sat for hours as self-righteous preachers thundered against the pleasures of the world. MacKenzie detested the rigid certainties and cant of Presbyterians. In Edinburgh, he never went to church on the Sabbath. Although attendance was compulsory, he ignored the summons. He had felt obliged to show face when younger, but he had lapsed after a few years. An elder had once demanded he go. He had refused politely, while cursing him in a stream of Gaelic invective. He was lucky as a well-to-do lawyer related to an earl. He could ignore the admonitions of elders below him in status. Other parishioners were not so lucky. They were forced to attend every week, sometimes dragged from their hearths to face the cold strictures of the reformed faith.

MacKenzie was directed to an office at the side of the church by a beadle. He knocked on the low door and opened it immediately. The minister Andrew Sharp was working at a desk. He did not look pleased to be interrupted.

Without raising his wigged head, Sharp snapped, 'What is it now, Spence?' before realising he was not speaking to the church official. 'I beg your pardon, sir. I'm trying to write my sermon. I've had too many interruptions already today.'

'I'll not keep you long, Mr Sharp. I am John MacKenzie.'

'I recognise you, sir.' Sharp put down his pen and eyed MacKenzie coldly.

'I was Clerk of the Session until recent changes. I have a few questions, if you'll allow me.' MacKenzie shut the door behind him. 'I'm working on a case for Dalrymple.'

'The killing of Mr Kerr?' the minister asked seriously, rising to shake MacKenzie's hand, before beckoning him to sit in front of the desk.

'The Advocate is so busy with parliamentary business, he's forced to employ me', said MacKenzie.

Sharp sat back and smiled. A look of self-righteousness spread across his face. 'These are historic days for this kingdom, Mr MacKenzie. We've waited long for deliverance from the yoke of Prelacy. We don't want anything upsetting the apple cart at the last moment. The Advocate does vital work. Parliament must establish presbytery on a legal basis.'

Sharp's arrogant tone got under MacKenzie's skin. He just could not contain his dislike of men of the cloth, especially followers of Calvin. 'What's the King's view of it all?' he asked, provocatively.

'You refer to King William, Mr MacKenzie?' Sharp asked gravely.

'Of course, Mr Sharp. I believe the previous incumbent struggles in exile.'

'King William looks favourably on it', said Sharp. 'He knows the existing religious settlement undermined the social harmony of the country, causing rebellion after rebellion in the south west. The King wants nothing to distract him from the struggle on the continent. The battle with Antichrist will be long and bloody. King Louis must be destroyed.' Sharp nodded to himself before continuing. 'The Scots do not like bishops, Mr MacKenzie. This land will not be at peace until they are sent packing.' Another self-satisfied smile lingered on Sharp's face.

'You may be right, Mr Sharp, but forcing clergy from their homes is surely unwise. A host of desperate curates now follow the Jacobites.'

'The people demand retribution for atrocities committed by Dundee. Many innocents were slain across Dumfriesshire and Galloway. The parishioners drive out those who sided with oppression. It's often the way at times of great change.'

MacKenzie smothered his anger by rubbing together the thumb and forefinger of his left hand. He felt himself relax and return the preacher's smile as he moved the conversation back to the matter at hand. There was no point in arguing about politics with a Presbyterian. 'As I was saying, Mr Sharp. I'm here regarding Jacob Kerr's death. I believe he was an elder?'

Sharp nodded grimly. 'A pious and long-serving one who attended the Session regularly. He was always a solid presence in our meetings. He did his duty and was an example to others.'

'How was he perceived in the Kirk?' MacKenzie asked.

'As a good, honest man, sir. As a hard-working merchant who had prospered in the cloth trade. As a devoted husband and father who led a quiet life in the service of the Lord. He did not seek office in the church but had to be persuaded to take the position of elder. He served God, quietly, humbly. He provided generous funds to charity. I believe he preferred a private life with his family.'

MacKenzie recalled the images of Kerr in the portraits in Van Diemen's Land. He found it difficult to equate the man described by the minister with the one on the walls of the house. 'Where did he stand in the church, Mr Sharp? Did he tend towards the fanatics?'

The minister shook his head, aggrieved by the question. 'I would not use that word to describe the more... enthusiastic of our church, sir. Kerr was not active in that way. He was not involved with any of the sectaries. He was a good, steady Presbyterian. He was staunchly anti-Papist, of course. He had no truck with Antichrist. I would put him firmly in the middle of the fold. Indeed, I believe I never heard him talk on the subject of church politics in all the years I knew him. He wanted presbytery and despised Papists like most Scots. He didn't need to say much more about it, nor did he.'

'What about his work in the Session? Was he active in rooting out sin in this parish?' asked MacKenzie.

The minister was about to reply but stopped himself for a moment and sat back, observing MacKenzie with displeasure. 'I don't like the tone of your questions, sir. Kerr was not the most vocal in the Session. As I've said, he attended regularly and rarely objected to decisions. In all the time I knew him, he always voted the same way as me. He was a loyal servant of the Session. He was a loyal servant of the Lord.'

'Then he might be described as a yes man', added MacKenzie, sardonically.

'He was, if you put it like that.' There was a hint of anger in Sharp's voice which rose in volume as he continued. 'He said yes to fighting blasphemy and yes to punishing sin. I would say, rather, he was an exemplary Christian who caused no man in this world any trouble. I've heard it said he always acted fairly in business. I've never heard a man say a bad word about him.'

'What about any woman?' asked MacKenzie, letting the question linger.

'I've never heard any woman ever mention him', replied Sharp after a few moments silence.

'So, he did not have enemies?

'I would say he had none. Unless a cloth deal soured sometime over the years. You must ask the merchants on the Exchange. I've heard of no strife over deals or anything related to business.'

MacKenzie's eyes drifted round the office, taking in the tall bookcases packed with dusty theological texts and a couple of paintings of preachers long departed. His eyes came to rest on a portrait of Andrew Melville, a famous minister from the earlier part of the century, who had challenged King James VI on the relationship between church and state. 'Can you think of any reason why Kerr would be killed so brutally, Mr Sharp?'

Sharp paused for a few moments. 'None at all. He lived an exemplary Christian life. I hear some sinner broke into his house during the night and killed him. It's a sign of the times, Mr MacKenzie. Evil is abundant in this kingdom; Satan's presence is palpable on the streets; all kinds of vice are prevalent in this city. Scepticism and atheism are openly voiced in coffee houses and taverns; witches are seen in the night sky. We approach the end of days, as foretold in the Bible, sir.'

MacKenzie smothered a desire to laugh at the nonsense coming from the preacher's mouth. He had a sudden realisation that they inhabited entirely separate intellectual universes. Why he found himself in one and Sharp in the other, however, he could not fathom. He continued with his questions. 'What about Kerr's wife and daughter, Mr Sharp?'

The minister had controlled his anger also. 'Godly creatures', he replied, smiling. 'His wife is a meek woman who obeyed her husband in all things; his daughter is a timid thing. They are exemplary members of the Kirk.'

MacKenzie felt he was getting nothing from the replies of the unctuous minister. 'I've heard Mrs Kerr and her daughter belong to a sisterhood of believers?'

Sharp eyed him suspiciously. 'They do, sir. What of it?'

'What is the function of such an assembly in the Kirk? How does such a group fit into a church organised around Kirk Sessions and presbyteries?'

Sharp appeared irritated again. 'There's no function, as you put it, unless it be to serve the Lord. They are just a group of women who come together outside regular times of worship. The women thirst for the Lord every day of the week, every minute of every hour, not just on the Sabbath.'

'Are such groups sanctioned officially by the Kirk?'

'Not exactly sanctioned. But they have not been discouraged. There's hunger among women for a greater role in serving the Lord. They like to interrogate ministers on theology. I can assure you they challenge us vigorously on our interpretation of the words of the Lord. They travel to hear preachers across the Lothians and Fife. Some of these associations were active in the opposition to the old King's regime. It may be different when presbytery is restored and the church returns to the path of righteousness. There will be less need for such enthusiasm then and the sisters may be discouraged. But until presbytery is enshrined in law, they are free to do as they want. Now, I must return to my sermon, Mr MacKenzie.'

MacKenzie continued, despite judging that Sharp wanted rid of him. 'Mrs Kerr, Mary Kerr and the maid Jane Montgomery are all members of Helen Sim's sisterhood?'

Sharp nodded. 'I've known Mrs Kerr for years. As I say, she is a pious creature. Her daughter is a timid girl. The maid is anxious to serve the Lord and vocal in her opposition to Antichrist.'

'Anxious to serve the Lord?' repeated MacKenzie. You often had to read between the lines when considering the words of Presbyterian ministers. They spoke in forked tongues.

'Some say she is too emotional in her prayer. She's more vivid a character than Mrs Kerr or her daughter. I would describe her as a vibrant, holy creature, but a godly one.'

MacKenzie began to rise, suggesting he was finished, but at the last moment dropped back into the seat and asked, 'Has there been anything of contention in the Session recently? Someone might have taken offence at a judgement and desired to harm Kerr?'

Sharp shook his head and impatiently sought a large leather-bound book on his desk which he flicked through. 'The Session minute book. I cannot think of anyone. There's nothing contentious in here, just a relentless record of sin: cases of fornication and cursing and swearing, and a recent case of blasphemy.'

'A case of blasphemy', repeated MacKenzie. Scougall, a devourer of the news sheets, usually kept him abreast of such things, but MacKenzie had spent most of his time at the Hawthorns since Geordie's birth and had missed the case.

'A student blasphemed against the Holy Trinity on the High Street. The case was sent to the higher authorities.'

'What was his name?' MacKenzie asked.

'Alexander Fraser was accused by five fellow students and found guilty by the Justiciary. He's incarcerated in the Tolbooth. He will be executed in a few days.'

'Did Kerr play any role in the Session? Did he question Fraser perhaps?'

Sharp looked down at the minute book and shook his head. 'Kerr said little during the interrogation.'

'I'll not keep you any longer from your sermon, Mr Sharp.' MacKenzie rose again and headed for the door. With his hand on the handle, he turned, his face adopting a stern expression. 'I have one last question, sir.'

'What is it, Mr MacKenzie? I'm a busy man.'

'To your knowledge, was Kerr a carnal man?'

A flash of fear was evident in the minister's eyes. 'What do you mean?'

'Was he known to have... lapses in his... moral life? Did Kerr have lapses from the godly life you describe?'

'What do you mean?' asked Sharp, bewildered.

'Did he visit prostitutes, Mr Sharp?'

Sharp looked upset by the question. 'I've no knowledge of it, sir. Why do you ask me this?'

MacKenzie glowered at Sharp as a wave of loathing rose in him for the hypocrisy of ministers. 'There is evidence suggesting such an interpretation. You have no knowledge of his appetites?'

'I'm sure he did not whore', Sharp replied angrily. 'He was an elder of the Kirk, Mr MacKenzie. You should not slander a dead man in such a way.'

'I do not slander him, sir. There is evidence of his... appetites.'

'What evidence do you refer to?' asked Sharp, defensively.

'I've examined Kerr's corpse, Mr Sharp.'

The minister looked disturbed.

'I've examined his member', continued MacKenzie. 'I would not say it is the tool of a celibate. Dr Lawtie will verify what I say. Kerr has suffered from the clap.'

Sharp looked shocked by the revelation. 'I did not know he was tortured by lust, sir.'

'He's not the first elder to condemn others for his own sin', said MacKenzie as he turned on his heels and left.

CHAPTER 7

A Pint with Thomas Cairns

WALKING BRISKLY DOWN the High Street, MacKenzie turned into Craigie's Pend, looking for Logan's Land, a tenement where Helen Sim worked as a seamstress. He carefully descended the stone steps to the basement and entered a tiny, low-ceilinged chamber where Sim, an old, stout woman with a mane of grey hair and deeply lined face, sat in the corner with needle and thread in hand.

She looked up expectantly from her work. 'What can I do for you, sir? A suit mended?'

MacKenzie nodded affably and introduced himself, taking the tiny chair she offered as she continued with her stitching. 'It's about the death of Mr Kerr, madam', he said.

She looked up at him suspiciously. 'Satan has visited Van Diemen's Land, sir. I'm sorry for it. Mr Kerr was an example to us all.'

'I believe you're acquainted with his wife and daughter.'

She nodded, dropping her eyes and continuing with her work. 'I've known them both for years. They are my beloved sisters in Christ. I also know their maid, Jane. They all worship the Lord with appetite. They all have hunger for the Lord, sir. As did Mr Kerr.'

'Can you think of any reason why Kerr was killed, Mrs Sim?' MacKenzie asked, mesmerised by the rapid movement of the old woman's hands.

'He was a man who served God every day of his life. So why would Satan visit his house? I don't know. The Lord's ways are mysterious. But everything will be made clear in good time. There will be some reason for it, only the Lord knows.'

'Was there unhappiness in the house?' asked MacKenzie.

She let the shirt she was mending rest on her lap, giving him a fierce look. 'What do you seek from me, Mr MacKenzie?' There was a flash of anger on her face. 'The Kerrs were good folk going about their own business', she said, before shaking her head and adding, 'We all suffer doubts but we can conquer them through prayer and worship of the Lord.'

'Do you mean Mr Kerr suffered from doubts?' MacKenzie asked.

She shook her head impatiently. 'No, I mean Mrs Kerr and Mary do. Mr Kerr may have suffered doubts, but I do not know about it.'

'What kind of doubts?'

'We are all tested by Satan, sir. Even the most devout who are secure in the arms of the Lord have doubts about whether they will enter Heaven at the end of days.'

'Religious doubts?' repeated MacKenzie.

'Doubts about God and the Devil', she said, frowning.

'What kind of doubts exactly, madam?' MacKenzie was not going to let the matter rest.

'Doubts caused by Satan. Doubts about the existence of the Lord. The fiend seeks to undermine belief by calling into question all that is good and holy. He tries to make us doubt the very existence of our Maker and Saviour. He encourages blasphemy which is the concomitant of disbelief. The devout can be afflicted by such thoughts which cause them great sorrow. Through long prayer and vibrant worship disbelief is nullified', she said nodding to herself.

'Both Mrs Kerr and Mary suffered in this way?' asked MacKenzie.

She continued to nod. 'It's common for the godly to be assaulted by Satan.'

'And did Jane suffer such thoughts?'

Sim nodded again and took up her sewing. 'I believe so, sir. Life is a struggle for those who follow the path of Christ. It is not the easy way. We must battle with sin continuously.'

MacKenzie took a few moments to look round the chamber. Mrs Sim lived a simple life with few possessions – a box bed, a couple of stools, a tiny table, a stove, a few cooking utensils, a couple of religious books and a Bible.

'Why did you start the sisterhood, madam?' he asked.

She put down her stitching again, this time on the table beside her chair and turned her full attention on him for the first time. 'I'll tell you why, sir. I had an aching desire in my soul to worship the Lord. I wanted to worship Him every minute of my life. A solitary sermon on the Sabbath was not enough for me. I wanted more. We came together to pray when we were not allowed to worship in kirks by Charles Stuart, called King by some. That is when it started. We found the countryside conducive to communion with the Lord. When we came together in the fields and beside rivers, we often found the Lord. When we travelled to hear worthy sermons in kirks across the land, we found the Lord. The sisterhood is about finding the Lord and about serving Him every hour of every day. Through such a life we can banish Satan. Tomorrow we journey to the Kirk at Cramond for a sermon. Why not come with us, Mr MacKenzie? Come and see how we are invigorated by the Lord. How we share the joy of communion with the Lord. I believe Mary, Jane and Mrs Kerr will all be there.'

'I think I'm too busy, Mrs Sim', said MacKenzie, smiling politely before continuing to question her. 'There's nothing you can tell me about any of them?'

She lifted the shirt from the table. 'I must be getting back to work, sir, if you'll excuse me. I cannot afford to spend all day in idle chatter.'

'What about Mary Kerr? She seems a timid girl?' asked MacKenzie, ignoring her hint that he should leave.

'She is quiet sometimes. But when the Holy Spirit enters her, she is as vibrant as the flowers in spring. She truly comes alive in the service of the Lord.'

'How did you find Mr Kerr, madam? Some were not taken with him.'

'He was always courteous with me, sir. I daresay those who were not taken with him were the godless scum in this city.'

'I will not take up any more of your time, Mrs Sim', said MacKenzie. He left a scribbled address on a piece of paper in case she thought of anything else pertinent to the case. He smiled to himself as he climbed out of the basement. He had an idea how Scougall might help him further.

Once in Cumming's Court, he tried the door of Cunningham's Land on the east side again. This time it was answered by a maid. She told him her master, Captain Burd, was away on a sea voyage to the Sound. MacKenzie recognised the name and realised the tenement belonged to Archibald Stirling's brother-in-law. The connection stopped him in his tracks and he stood before her lost in thought for a few moments, reflecting on the haunting power of the past. His life had been busy since his old friend's death the year before. What he would give for a round of golf or a night at cards with him. He missed Stirling's intense cynicism during days when a deluge of hypocrisy rained on the city. He could hear Stirling's voice speaking to him inside his head. 'Let me tell you of Montrose, John. Let me tell you what Montrose would've done.' Montrose, who led the King's cause in Scotland during the civil wars, had been Stirling's hero.

MacKenzie came back to himself and smiled at the maid. Stirling would have loved the present case. He was always amused by the hypocrisy of men of God.

'Do you know about the death next door?' he asked her.

She nodded nervously. 'The master's hardly here, sir. I attend the house only once a week to keep it tidy. I do not stay here. The master's son visits sometimes. He has a house in the Canongate.'

'Do you know anything about the Kerr family?'

She shook her head. 'Only to greet them on the street; I've never been in the house. I've heard they are a holy family. It's terrible what's happened, sir.'

'Have you ever heard anything inside the house? Have you ever heard cries or screams?' asked MacKenzie, earnestly.

She looked surprised by the question. 'Nothing of that kind, sir. Never.'

He thanked her and returned to Van Diemen's Land where Jane answered the door. MacKenzie noticed dark hair pulled up under her mutch. He smiled affably at her. 'Please tell your mistress I want to speak with her again.'

Jane showed him into the living chamber and he took a seat in the same finely upholstered chair he had sat on the day before. Mrs Kerr appeared a few minutes later, looking less distraught than the previous day.

'Have you found out anything about my husband's killer, Mr MacKenzie?' she asked urgently as she approached him.

MacKenzie indicated she should sit and he fumbled in his pocket for his pipe which he held up to her apologetically. 'Do you mind if I smoke, madam? I'm sorry, a vile habit, I know, but it helps me think.'

She shook her head. He set his pipe alight and was soon puffing away. She sat, drawing her knees together and placing her hands in her lap, turning her nose away from the smoke drifting across the room. 'My husband did not approve of tobacco', she said, blankly, but with no indication from the tone of her statement whether she shared her husband's view.

'I need to ask a few more questions, madam', began MacKenzie. 'Some of them will be harder for you than the ones yesterday.'

She nodded and turned to look at him.

'You'll not like me for asking them but I must. We are dealing with a savage killing.'

She nodded. 'Then you do not think it was theft?'

MacKenzie leaned forwards on his knees and stared intently at her. It was a tactic he had often used in court as a lawyer to intimidate those he was questioning. A slight invasion of a person's space could put them on the defensive. 'I may come back to that, madam. But first tell me, honestly, how were relations between you and your husband?'

She looked down at her hands again, caught off guard by the direct question. 'What do you mean, sir?' she stammered.

'Was your marriage a happy one? Was your marriage a contented one? Was Mr Kerr a good husband?' MacKenzie fired the questions out, one after the other.

She looked upset. 'I don't like to discuss such things with a stranger. We were married 20 years for God's sake... happily.'

'Were relations between your husband and daughter good?' MacKenzie continued to probe.

'What are you getting at, Mr MacKenzie! I thought you sought a thief. I did not think you came into this house to delve into our private life. It is no one's business but our own.'

MacKenzie sat back and sucked on his pipe, eyeing her carefully. 'I must delve deeply into this house, madam, much more deeply. It's possible someone in this house was involved in the killing of your husband.'

She looked up, startled. 'Why do you say that, sir?'

'For one simple reason, madam. The debris from the broken lock was inside the door and the weather on the night your husband died was calm. The pieces could not have been blown in by the wind. In addition, there were marks made by a tool around the lock on the inside of the door. In other words, it's likely the door was forced from the inside rather than outside. Is that not strange, madam?'

'Why on earth would someone do that?' she asked.

'For one simple reason – to make it look like somebody had broken into the house. To make it look like Mr Kerr was killed by a thief.'

'What about the kist?' she asked, defensively.

'To make it look like robbery – when, in fact, it was nothing of the sort.'

She got to her feet with panic on her face and paced back and forward across the room, her arms crossed protectively over her chest. After a minute or so, she stopped and turned to him, looking agitated. 'Then the killer may be behind these walls! I cannot believe Agnes or Jane could do such a thing.'

'Please remain calm, madam. It does not necessarily mean the killer is a member of your household. The killer was perhaps let into the house or found a way of getting in. I don't know yet. But I must ask again: how were relations between you and your husband?'

She said nothing, but stood at the fire staring into the hearth, her back to him.

MacKenzie continued to question her as she stood there. 'This may be difficult for you, madam. I'm afraid I must ask it. The postmortem has revealed your husband was... diseased.'

'Diseased?' she asked, turning towards him, confused.

'He had suffered from a venereal complaint in the past. Did he visit prostitutes, madam?'

She left the fire and began to pace back and forwards across the room again. At last she sat down and spoke in a tearful whisper. 'In the past... years ago... he confessed to me... just after we were married. He wanted us both to be completely honest with each other. He told me he was tortured by lust as a young man. But it was long time ago. It was a time of weakness when he was tempted by the Devil. Through worship of the Lord and continuous prayer, he conquered the vile sin of lust.'

MacKenzie's grim expression did not alter. 'I'm sorry to ask you, madam. It's of course a sensitive matter, as your husband was an elder. I'm not saying elders never visit brothels, but when it emerges into the light of day, there's often a desire among people to learn about it for purely salacious reasons. The *Gazette* may want to publish a story about it.'

She dropped her head into her hands. 'I'm sure he ceased such things. He was troubled as a young man. He was tempted by Satan. But he conquered his desires. He fought Satan, vehemently. He prayed, relentlessly, for relief. I would have known if he still went to such places. I would have known if he had... other women. I know he conquered lust through prayer!'

MacKenzie nodded thoughtfully and rose himself, going to the fire to empty his pipe. After refilling it and lighting it, he returned to the chair before continuing. 'A neighbour has heard cries and screams from your house during the night.'

She stood up again and her composure drained away. 'My God, are we the talk of the town! What house cannot claim some unhappiness at times? We all struggle... we all struggle with sin... we all... we are all punished for our sins... we all experience times of doubt... but we pray. We are aided by the Lord in our fight against Satan. With prayer we can conquer everything.'

MacKenzie was surprised by her sudden outburst and waited for her to regain her equanimity. She sat back and bowed her head. 'You're right, madam', he said. 'We're all afflicted sometimes. But this is something specific and recurring, described as the awful cries of a girl, as if she was being tortured.'

Mrs Kerr rubbed her hands as if trying to clean something off them and looked away as she spoke softly. 'He did beat the child sometimes. That must be that what was heard. Thomas wailed at night in his chamber like a girl. The punishment was no more severe than any master would treat a servant. He deserved it for his forgetfulness.'

'Agnes' boy?' asked MacKenzie.

'Yes. He was naughty, sometimes, and beaten by my husband for it. Spare the rod and spoil the child. The boy would go to bed in tears and wake in the night. He would scream and wake us all with his wailing.'

'What of the girl's cries?'

'It was the boy's. He sounded like a girl. He would blubber away in his bed.'

MacKenzie's eyes wandered round the room and came to rest on Kerr's portrait. Jacob Kerr did not look like a gentle man. MacKenzie pitied anyone who had to take a beating from him. 'Was your husband a cruel man, madam?'

She took time to reply, as if gathering her emotions and smothering them. 'No crueller than the next. My husband fought the Devil. He would pray for hours on the Sabbath. He got down on his knees on the floor of our chamber. All of us in the house could hear him. He fought Satan every day of his life. He struggled with sin. We could hear his battles. But he vanquished the Devil.'

'What about your daughter, madam. Was she ever beaten?' MacKenzie continued, calmly, sensing he was beginning to peel back the outer layers of an onion. But what would he find at the centre?

'Only when she was a child, and then rarely. He has not struck her for years.'

'What about Agnes and Jane?'

'Why would he beat them?' She looked surprised by the question.

'I do not know why, madam. I simply ask if he beat them.'

She thought for a moment, looking blankly away. 'Agnes, yes, maybe years ago, when she was young. Agnes was little more than a girl when she started with us. She had to be reprimanded and beaten sometimes. Jane is a God-fearing girl, strong in her devotion to the Lord who works hard in the house. There was never any reason to punish her.'

MacKenzie put down his pipe and let his stern expression drop as suddenly as it had appeared. 'Thank you, Mrs Kerr.'

He asked to speak with Mary. Mrs Kerr went to fetch her. Mary entered and sat nervously. MacKenzie saw she was shaking. He knew instinctively there was something going on in the house he was not being told about. There was something more than mourning a dead father. He decided it was time to adopt a more strident approach. He dropped his mask of affability and adopted the role of advocate. He knew she would be shocked by the change but it was necessary. He did not smile at her as he had the day before, but stared intently, waiting a couple of minutes without speaking to unnerve her. Then the tone of his voice sharpened. 'I want you to tell me the truth today, Mary. I've had enough of the lies in this house.'

He waited to see her reaction. She did not meet his eyes but kept looking down at her hands in her lap, which continued to shake. He noticed a gold ring around a skeletal finger.

'I want you tell me the truth, Mary. You know I act with the authority of the Lord Advocate. What you say to me will be heard by God. Tell me, did your father mistreat anyone in this house?'

There was silence. Only the distant sounds on the High Street were audible. She did not look up. She did not answer.

He waited another minute, staring at her, letting the silence linger. 'Did your father beat the boy?'

No answer. She shook her head.

'Did he mistreat Jane?'

The same again.

'Did he mistreat your mother or Agnes?'

She shook her head. She closed her eyes tightly. She was still shaking. She seemed to be murmuring something under her breath. He realised she was praying.

He raised his voice further. 'Did he mistreat you? For God's sake, girl, answer me!'

She broke down in tears and screamed out, 'I have nothing to say about him. Nothing!'

MacKenzie rose to his feet and went over to her, looming above her, trying to scare the truth out of her. She looked up at him, an expression of utter terror on her face. Suddenly she jumped up out of the chair and made to leave. MacKenzie grabbed her arm to stop her. As he did so, her sleeve rose up her lower arm and he saw something on her skin. He held her tightly and pulled the sleeve up to the elbow. There were marks across her wrists and up her forearm. He yanked the other sleeve up. It was the same. Tears were on her cheeks. She was whimpering like a puppy and struggling to get away from him. Her bonnet was dislodged slightly, revealing blonde locks on one side. Both her arms were a mass of scars, like the lattice of pastry on top of an apple pie.

'Who did this to you, Mary? Who would do this to you?' His anger was gone and he asked sympathetically.

She shook her head again.

'Who did this to you?' His voice dropped to an insistent whisper. 'Was it your father? Was it punishment by your father?'

She shook her head violently. 'It was not him!' she screamed.

'Then who did it? For God's sake, tell me, girl!'

She finally looked him straight in the eyes with burning hatred. 'I did it. I cut myself! I had to cut myself', she burst out. 'I had to cut the Devil out of me. I had to cut him out, when he tempted me. When he came to me and told me to sin. I had to cut him out with the blade of a knife! Here and here and here.' She indicated with her hand across her forearms in a cutting motion.

MacKenzie let go of her. She turned and ran out the room in tears. He had a sudden epiphany, recalling his own melancholia over the years. Although he had never been tempted to cut himself, he had felt the irresistible pull of the loaded pistol. Countless times he had been tempted by the gun in his desk drawer. Something had always held him back – usually the thought of his daughter left alone in the world.

He took out his pipe and lit it, standing for a few minutes at the window, looking down on the courtyard beneath. He turned and went to look for Agnes in the kitchen. He heard her before he could see her, working at the kitchen table, chopping and slicing vegetables. She put her knife down as he entered.

'You gave me a fright, Mr MacKenzie. I didn't know you were back in the house. Have you caught him yet?' Agnes looked like she had recovered from the shock of the day before. It was back to business for her. There were dishes to prepare. The family still had to eat.

'Not yet, Agnes. I've a few more questions for you.'

'For me?' she asked surprised. She wiped her hands on her apron and put the knife down carefully.

MacKenzie looked at the implement resting on the wooden block on the table. A similar weapon had slain Kerr. Where was the weapon now? It could be at the bottom of the Nor Loch or dumped in one of Edinburgh's middens. Or it could still be in the house, hidden somewhere. The same could be said for the documents taken from the smaller kist if they were removed by someone in the house to make it look like theft. He stood at the other side of the table on the spot where Kerr's body had lain the day before. 'Did Mr Kerr mistreat your boy, Agnes?' he asked.

She was taken aback by the question. She shook her head.

'Did he beat him beyond what would be regarded as reasonable?'

'I do not think so, sir. He did beat him, of course. It was no more than any other boy received. Thomas can be forgetful when sent for messages. He wanders off to play sometimes. He does not return for hours. If that happened, if he forgot what he was sent for, if he returned empty-handed, he was punished like any child. He did not like it, but it was necessary. I did not like to see him beaten by the master but I know it was necessary.'

MacKenzie leant forward, putting his hands down on the table, straight across from her. 'So you would not say Kerr was cruel to him?'

'No, sir. He was a… good master… to me and him. I've told you already. He provided us with food and shelter and work and he promised a future for Thomas.'

'Did Kerr ever strike you, Agnes? I want you to tell me the truth.' He stared intently at her.

She looked unsettled by the question and brushed down her apron again. 'No, he did not, sir. He was a good master.

He was fair. Always fair. And devout. We heard him praying to the Lord, sometimes for the whole of the Sabbath in his room. He was praying down on his knees without food or water all day. We heard him praying for hours alone in the room, beseeching the Lord for forgiveness, fighting Satan with prayer.'

'Forgiveness for what?'

'We are all sinners are we not, sir? Each day we sin in our thoughts.'

'What of Mary and Mrs Kerr? Did he ever strike them?'

'I never saw him do it. He didn't take any nonsense from them. Mary was scared of him, but she respected him as head of the household.' Agnes closed her eyes and bowed her head for a moment before opening them and continuing more calmly. 'We lived well here, sir. We lived a quiet life behind these walls. A quiet life until... this happened.'

MacKenzie was getting tired of the wall of silence. He sighed. 'Then tell me this, Agnes. Why would Mary cut her arms?' He opened his palms to her and indicated where she cut herself on the forearms. 'Why would she cut her arms until they bled and left scars? Why would she do that?'

'Cut herself? What do you mean, sir?'

'You must've seen her arms. They are slashed all the way up to her elbows. She must have some great... unhappiness.'

'She's a strange girl, sir. She's a sad girl. Some are born like that. I never knew she did such a thing. I wonder if she was told to by the sisters. They are an odd brood. Was she trying to cut her sins out of her body? I've heard girls cut the Devil out when tempted by sin, when they have dreams of lust or desire to fornicate. By cutting themselves, they hope the desire to sin will cease.'

'Where is your son, Agnes?'

'He's doing a message for the mistress. He'll be back soon.'

MacKenzie returned to the ground floor to examine Kerr's merchandise again and then climbed to the second floor. He knocked on the door of Mrs Kerr's bed chamber and when there was no answer he entered, closing the door behind him. He went to the far side of the bed and got down on his hands and knees. The chamber pot on that side was now empty and the floor around it washed. He moved it to the side and began to test the floorboards. One wobbled slightly. He got his fingers round the edge of it and lifted it up. Underneath was a rag. He picked it up carefully. The rag opened to reveal a small knife. It was a kitchen knife with a blade about four inches long. He examined the handle. It was the same as the handles of the other knives in the kitchen. It was surely the weapon used to kill Kerr. He wrapped it in the rag again and lowered it gently into his jacket pocket, before leaving the house. He walked down Cockburn's Wynd, deep in thought, to wait where the wynd joined the High Street. The weapon was hidden in Mrs Kerr's chamber. Did this mean she had killed her husband or was she protecting another member of the household?

MacKenzie stood, watching the passers-by, listening to conversations about Ireland and how the Jacobites would be crushed by King William's army, a vast force made up of soldiers from all over Europe. He was struck by the thought that great historical events were happening at that very moment elsewhere, events which would shape the future of Scotland, England and Ireland, while he was concerned with the tragic happenings in an Edinburgh household. The events in Van Diemen's Land seemed unconnected to those in Ireland. But were they? Kerr had been no Jacobite. That was certain.

He took out his pipe and filled it, standing statuesque at the entrance of the vennel, puffing away. He looked back at the door of Van Diemen's Land. Behind it lived four women and a boy. Were any of them involved in Kerr's killing or were they all involved? Or was someone else, an outsider, let into the house to kill him for one of them? Or for some other reason? He spotted Thomas sauntering up the High Street towards him. The boy was surely too small to murder a man of Kerr's size himself, but with his mother's help could they have contrived it together?

MacKenzie waved as the boy approached. 'Hello, Thomas. I've a message from your mother', he lied.

Thomas looked up at him fearfully.

'Don't be afraid, Thomas. She wants a leg of mutton from the Flesher's Market.'

Thomas looked surprised but not displeased. It would mean he could spend more time on the streets. He would be away from Van Diemen's Land for longer.

'I'll walk down with you, if you don't mind. I'm going that way, anyway', added MacKenzie.

Thomas nodded and turned on his heels. They walked back down the busy High Street through the crowds, past the high tenements of the Lawnmarket towards St Giles Kirk on the right. MacKenzie had a good look at the boy on the way. Thomas appeared well-nourished and in good health. He did not look badly treated. 'Do you know your letters?' MacKenzie asked him casually as they came to the Luckenbooths.

'I do, sir. Jane is teaching me.'

'Why does Jane help you?' MacKenzie asked.

'She knows how to read and write, while mother does not. Mother started work when she was 12, so she never learned. I will make a clerk someday, mother says. That's what I hope to be, sir. I want to make my way in the world as a writer.'

'It's a worthy profession', MacKenzie smiled at Thomas' innocent ambition. 'If you continue well in your studies, I might help to find you a place as an apprentice notary. You might rise through the profession. Have a home of your own someday. You and your mother would not have to live in Van Diemen's Land any longer. Would you like that, Thomas?'

The boy nodded eagerly. 'Yes, sir. I would like a place of my own.'

'Do you not like living in Van Diemen's Land?' MacKenzie asked.

Thomas thought for a moment, looking puzzled. 'I did not like it, sir. But it's all right now.'

'Why is that, Thomas?'

He did not answer.

'Why is that, Thomas?' MacKenzie repeated, more insistently.

'I cannot say it, sir.'

'You can tell me, Thomas. I keep the confidence of my clients as an advocate. You might one day become an advocate yourself and plead in the Court of Session. You might make money for your mother. She would no longer have to be a servant. You would not have to rely on the Kerr family in Van Diemen's Land. And besides, I'm your friend, Thomas. You can trust me.' MacKenzie stopped him by placing his hand on his shoulder.

Thomas relaxed. 'I just meant it's… easier in the house since the master is gone.'

'Was he a demanding master? I know he was not pleased when you forgot your messages.'

The boy nodded.

'Tell me, Thomas. Did Mr Kerr beat you badly?'

They were standing at the entry of Flesher's Close beside the Tron Kirk where the noise of the Flesher's Market was audible, accompanied by the pungent smell of blood and flesh.

'You can tell me, Thomas. He cannot hurt you anymore. You'll not be beaten anymore. Tell me what he did to you.'

'Mother told me never to say anything. She said to say nothing about the master to anyone', he replied nervously.

'I'll not tell her anything, if you tell me what he did to you, Thomas. I need to find out the truth about what happened in Van Diemen's Land. That's not a bad thing, is it, discovering the truth?'

The boy shook his head. 'He... he...', he stammered, looking suddenly petrified. 'He told me if I sinned the Devil would take me. He had to whip me to remind me my eternal soul was in danger. He had to beat the Devil out of me. Mother could not stop him. He would beat me for the slightest thing.' He untucked his shirt and raised it a few inches to reveal a large purple bruise across his stomach. 'He kicked me, sir. He kicked me when I lay on the ground.' MacKenzie shook his head, recalling the portraits of Kerr in Van Diemen's Land. The artist never lied, he thought. The Dutchman had portrayed him as a dark presence. But was Kerr's brutality connected to his death?

'It's over now, Thomas. Come, I'll take you for a pint in Penstoun's. You can tell me everything there.'

The boy did not argue. He followed MacKenzie obediently down the High Street past the Tron Kirk and into the narrow entrance of a wynd on the left. They entered an alehouse and took a table. Thomas sipped his ale as MacKenzie smoked and drank a glass of wine. After a few minutes, MacKenzie continued to question him. 'Did he ever beat your mother, Thomas?'

The boy looked around furtively, then nodded. 'If he did not like the food she prepared or if the kitchen was untidy. He would send me to my room or for a message. He would take off his belt. It had a big buckle on it. He would whip her with it. Once I hid behind the door and watched him. I tried to stop him but he turned it on me and whipped me black and blue. I was not allowed out the house until the marks were gone from my body.' There was a look of terror on Thomas' face as he recalled the memory.

MacKenzie shook his head in disgust. 'I'm sorry you've both suffered so much in his house.' He sat back, puffing on his pipe, allowing Thomas to sip his ale, pleased by the feeling he was getting somewhere with the investigation at last. After a few minutes, he asked him, 'Did he do other things to your mother, Thomas? Do you know what I mean by the question? Did he ever lie with her against her will?'

Thomas nodded, knowingly. MacKenzie noticed a tear on the boy's cheek. 'He has not done it in a long time', he replied in a whisper, looking vacantly across the tavern. 'He came to our chamber at night when I was a bairn. The sounds he made woke me up. The first time I thought a beast was attacking mother in bed. It was all grunting and swearing and cursing. I thought the Devil was on top of her. She always cried afterwards. I hated him.'

'He will never trouble you or your mother again, Thomas', MacKenzie sighed. He let the boy take some more ale, before asking, 'Did he also beat his bedfellow?'

Thomas finished the pint of ale. 'I never saw him do it, sir. But I heard her crying often in her chamber. It scared me to hear her cry in that way.'

MacKenzie did not want to push him further. He was getting more of the truth from him than from all the women in the house. He continued in a relaxed tone. 'What about Mary?'

'I don't know if he beat her, sir. But I've heard her crying in her room also. Mary is very sad. I try to make her smile by telling her jokes. But she hardly ever laughs. She hardly eats anything. She just picks at her food.'

'What about Jane?'

'I do not know, sir.'

'You're all better off with him dead, Thomas. He was more of a devil than a man', MacKenzie said, shaking his head.

Thomas did not reply immediately. He looked on the verge of saying something else, but stopped himself. 'I must go now, sir. I'll have to place the order with the fleshers. They'll be looking for me back home.'

'Don't worry, Thomas, I'll place the order for you. I'm going that way anyway. Just one last thing. Do not tell anyone I've spoken to you until the crime is solved. Let this chat be our little secret. Don't even tell your mother. In return, I'll not tell her about the pint of ale.' MacKenzie winked and gave the boy a friendly nudge with his elbow.

MacKenzie headed up the Lawnmarket slowly, turning over in his mind the pieces of evidence he had gathered: the fragment of cloth, the empty kist, the broken lock, the hair under the kitchen table and the knife in Mrs Kerr's chamber. There was also Mary's self-harm, the beatings suffered by Agnes and Thomas and the screams during the night. He turned right into Merton's Close and entered the Periwig. Scougall was waiting for him at their usual table, nursing a cup of ale. 'I can only stay a short while, sir. Chrissie's preparing a venison pie', Scougall said anxiously.

'I'll not keep you from your pie, Davie. Let's share a quick bottle. It will aid your digestion. As we say in Gaelic, wine is the best accompaniment of any dish.'

'I'll stick with this, if you don't mind, sir', said Scougall, raising his tankard.

MacKenzie shook his head in disgust at the watery ale. 'Did you find out anything about Kerr?' he asked, after calling for a bottle of burgundy.

'I asked my colleagues in the office and acquaintances in the Exchange and around the Luckenbooths. They all had the same story to tell. Kerr was a quiet man who pursued his business in a reasonable way. He was a reluctant member of the Session but attended regularly. No one knew him particularly well. He had no close friends. He kept himself to himself. That was all.' Scougall placed a nervous hand on his hat. 'Is there anything else you want, sir? I really must be leaving.'

'What did Chrissie make of the piece of cloth?'

Scougall reached in his pocket, took out the fabric and handed it to MacKenzie. 'She thinks it's a piece of cotton from a shirt or shift.'

MacKenzie nodded thoughtfully. 'Thank her, Davie. One last thing. I missed news of the blasphemy case.'

Scougall grimaced. 'A student called Alexander Fraser was overheard blaspheming outside the Tron Kirk. The case was passed from the Session to the Justiciary. A number of Fraser's fellow students testified against him. He was found guilty and will hang in a matter of days. Some of the more enthusiastic ministers whip up their parishioners. The family hope for a reprieve from the Privy Council, but it doesn't look hopeful.' Scougall hesitated for a moment before adding, 'The punishment is extreme if you ask me, sir. He should be humiliated before the parish but the ministers want his blood.'

'It's a dreadful case, Davie. I hope the Council show leniency.'

Scougall took up his hat again. 'Is there anything more, sir?'

MacKenzie patted him gently on the arm and smiled. 'Just one other favour, Davie.'

CHAPTER 8

A Sermon in Cramond Kirk

SCOUGALL WAS SURPRISED by Chrissie's enthusiastic response to MacKenzie's request that they attend a sermon in Cramond on the Sabbath. It was a chance to observe Mrs Kerr, her daughter and maid among the sisterhood, MacKenzie argued. Having shared all he knew about the case, Scougall was a little surprised by how much interest Chrissie showed in the details of the killing.

'We must play a role, Chrissie', he said as they lay in bed the night before. 'We must play the role of devout Presbyterians. It's not that I'm not devout myself, of course, but we must not give any hint of the true reason we're going to Cramond. I don't like deceiving anyone... but investigating a murder sometimes requires a little... guile.' Scougall could sense Chrissie's excitement and he could not help feeling slightly self-important.

'Who's the minister there, Davie?' she asked, nestling into his shoulder, and looking up at him with her dark brown eyes.

Scougall was still not used to sharing his bed. Every time he got under the sheets, he would close his eyes and thank God for his good fortune. He looked down at the curve of her body under the blankets and felt the beginnings of arousal. 'Alexander Smeaton. He's known for his long sermons.'

'How will we know the Kerr family?' she asked.

'MacKenzie described Mrs Kerr to me. Her daughter and maid will accompany her. We should be able to identify them easily enough.'

'I look forward, to it, Davie', smiled Chrissie with a twinkle in her eye. 'The sermon of Mr Smeaton, I mean, of course.'

They rose early next morning and, after a quick breakfast of salted porridge prepared expertly by Chrissie, joined the worshippers, just after dawn, outside St Giles Kirk. There were about 25 altogether, an assortment of ages, mostly women of the sisterhood, joined by a few husbands and brothers, all dressed conservatively in black. Scougall identified Mrs Kerr and pointed her out to Chrissie. Two young women stood beside her, one hanging on each arm. The thin one must be her daughter Mary, thought Scougall. The other must be Jane. She was younger with darker skin and a fuller figure. Scougall shared his thoughts with Chrissie in a nervous whisper. He was feeling awkward. Such undercover work did not suit him. Chrissie nodded and held on to his arm tightly.

A man passing on the street stopped beside them and unexpectedly addressed him. 'Mr Scougall is it not, sir?' he asked in a friendly manner.

Scougall was surprised and speechless, not recognising him.

'I am Hugh Umpherston, sir. Do you do not remember me?'

Scougall observed him carefully.

'You prepared an instrument for me a couple of years ago', continued Umpherston. 'I've lost a hair or two since then.' He smiled as he raised his hat to reveal a bald head.

Scougall recalled him at last. Umpherston had indeed lost his hair and put on more than a few pounds in weight since they had last met. 'Of course, I'm sorry, Mr Umpherston.'

'I live in Glasgow now but I'm back to see my brother. He's over there with his wife and daughter. I agreed to go with them to Cramond. A day at the seaside they told me. I might slip off if the sermon's too long and take the air by the shore.' He gave Scougall a sly wink and suggested, by a tipping movement of his hand, he would seek refuge in a tavern. 'I only agreed to come to please my sister-in-law. It's not my kind of thing. But they are enthusiastic about it all.'

Scougall remembered Umpherston as a friendly, boisterous, apprentice who enjoyed late-night boozing. He was surely the most unlikely person to meet in such company. He introduced him to Chrissie. 'We seek something interesting, something thought provoking. We've heard Mr Smeaton's sermons are... enlightening', said Scougall, trying not to sound too pompous.

'And long, Mr Scougall!' Umpherston laughed. 'They're an eager group all right, very enthusiastic about religion, dedicated to serving the Lord.' He smiled broadly and turned to look at Chrissie, eyeing her up and down without subtlety, which was not lost on her husband who experienced a flash of jealousy.

'I don't know much about them, Mr Umpherston. We come to hear a good sermon. What is the sisterhood all about?' asked Chrissie, adopting the role of eager Presbyterian with ease, and helping out her tongue-tied husband.

'My sister-in-law belongs to them, Mrs Scougall', began Umpherston, taking the opportunity to move closer to Chrissie. 'It's a sight to see them all praying together in a field. Some get right carried away with it all. They say the Holy Spirit enters them. Sometimes it goes on for hours. They can reach a fair state of excitement. You'd think they'd been for a turn in the hay with a lad.' Umpherston laughed loudly attracting the attention of a couple of frowning sisters standing nearby.

'Do you know Mrs Kerr and her family?' asked Chrissie, taking over from Scougall, who was still pondering whether he should reprimand Umpherston for being too forward with his wife.

'My sister-in-law knows them. I would describe the Kerrs as real enthusiasts. They are quiet enough when you meet them on the street. But, my God, are they hungry for the Lord. They're a different kettle of fish at a conventicle. You'll see what I mean if they stop on the way. I was shocked to hear what happened to Jacob Kerr.' Umpherston turned to look at Mrs Kerr. 'She's a handsome woman and now an eligible one', he continued. 'Although perhaps a year or two older than I'm looking for! Ah, we're leaving now... We'll speak later, Mr Scougall, Mrs Scougall. Enjoy the walk.'

Scougall shook his head in disapproval when Umpherston had gone and they joined the back of the procession as it snaked its way down Leith Wynd and out of the city to follow the north road across the Water of Leith at Stockbridge, before winding north-west.

It was a bright spring morning and Scougall was happy to take his wife's hand as they walked along, chatting idly. Chrissie looked up at him, now and again, to give him a sly wink. It was all great fun for her, he thought. He thanked God that after his travails with women in the past, God had rewarded him with Chrissie. He could not help thinking he didn't deserve such a bonnie wife. Chrissie talked most of the way in a playful fashion, keeping off the subject of Van Diemen's Land, asking Scougall about his office and other things, like should she take up the game of golf. Was it not true that Mary Queen of Scots was a keen player? It was a running joke between them. She had no intention of playing a game she viewed as tiresome, while Scougall took particular pleasure in explaining the rules to her, which she had completely forgotten by the next time she asked.

After walking for an hour and a half, they stopped to rest. Some of the party ate their refreshments, pieces of bread and cheese or a pie, and drank the fresh water from a stream. Others, including the Kerrs, wandered off into the surrounding rigs. Scougall took Chrissie's hand and guided her to a rock on which they could sit and munch their pieces while watching everyone around them.

A tiny old woman raised her arms and began to pray fervently. Scougall presumed it was Helen Sim as she fitted MacKenzie's description. She called on the Lord to guide them through the valley of sin. The other sisters formed a small circle around her, including Mrs Kerr, Mary, Jane and a couple of other young women. They all had their eyes closed with arms raised to the sky. When Mrs Sim had finished, Mrs Kerr began to pray even more fervently, pouring her heart out to the Lord.

Her words carried across to them in the breeze: 'Turn us from sin, oh Lord. Set us on the straight path to salvation, oh Lord. Let not sin stain the white linen of our souls. Bring to light all evil within this land. Cast evil and sin from our lives. Let us not be led astray by Satan. We will fight him each day with your help, oh Lord, even though he lives among us in our house, we will fight him with your love. Pray for our poor departed bedfellow so he be taken up into the arms of Christ and cleansed of his sins. Amen!'

She opened her eyes and turned to her daughter. Mary looked back coldly, closed her eyes and began to call out in a high, bird-like voice, suddenly invigorated. 'Oh Lord save us all from sin... guide us through this valley of despair...' She went on for a couple of minutes. There were tears on her cheeks as she turned to Jane, who continued in similar fashion. 'You are the love and light of our lives, oh Lord. Help us overcome the strife afflicting us.'

And then one of the others who had joined them began to pray in a deeper, more sonorous voice, the words striking Scougall with their vigour: 'We will fight Antichrist in all his guises. We will slay Satan with prayer and with the love of God…' Finally, they called Amen together and smiled at each other, taking each other's hands and kissing them.

Scougall suddenly thought he should have recorded everything in shorthand for MacKenzie. He had forgotten he was there to observe, struck as he was by the power of their devotion. He also felt annoyed that cynicism stained his own views and recalled the days of his youth when he was untroubled by any doubts and would have shared their fervency.

The party of sisters returned to the road, passing close to the rock where Scougall and Chrissie were sitting. Mrs Kerr smiled at them warmly. 'Good day to you, sir, madam. It's a fine day, indeed. Are you going all the way to Cramond to hear Mr Smeaton?'

Scougall had not expected he would have to speak to any of the party and he was lost for words, fearful that he might divulge something about his friendship with MacKenzie or knowledge of the events in Van Diemen's Land. His face reddened and he could not think of anything to say. Fortunately, Chrissie intervened to save him further embarrassment, replying calmly, 'We look forward to it much, madam. I am Chrissie Scougall and this is my husband Davie, notary in the city. We've not heard Mr Smeaton preach before.'

The words 'This is my husband Davie' gave Scougall a warm feeling and he smiled sheepishly at Mrs Kerr. 'I hear he's a fine preacher, madam', he added. It was all he could think of saying.

'I am Margaret Kerr and this is my daughter Mary and servant Jane.'

'We are sorry for your loss, madam', said Scougall, remembering she was a recent relict.

'Thank you', she replied, before continuing, 'The Lord smites Satan with wise words, Mr Scougall. Mr Smeaton will have much to say about these days of shame we live through and our hopes for the return of presbytery. I hope you both find the Lord.'

Scougall observed them at close quarters, remembering the example of MacKenzie. Mrs Kerr appeared dignified in her grief, although he judged not overcome by it as he might have expected a widow of a couple of days. Mary Kerr was a thin, nervous girl who kept looking down at the ground, and did not meet his eyes. Jane Montgomery looked more confident, meeting his gaze as he looked at her. She was a girl of similar age, a pretty thing with a coquettish look.

They continued to Cramond Kirk with its squat tower at the confluence of the River Almond and the Firth of Forth. Early for the sermon, they had to daunder in the kirkyard, Scougall keeping a close eye on the Kerrs. Mother, daughter and maid stood silently together.

The sermon began at eleven o'clock. By then, the church was full, the local parishioners of Cramond swelled by the party from Edinburgh and other similar groups from surrounding towns. There was an atmosphere of anticipation as they awaited the arrival of Smeaton. Scougall and Chrissie sat near the back, a few rows behind the Kerrs. When the minister entered, the church fell silent at the sound of his crisp steps on the flagstones as he approached the lectern. Smeaton was a young, dashing figure in long, black robes.

Without hesitation, he launched into his sermon confidently, not looking down at the notes he had placed in front of him. 'This nation is bonded with sin. This nation is bonded with sin. Sin clings to this nation like clart on the wheel of a wagon. Sin is like ivy on the tree of the world. How can we free ourselves from this thing called sin? How can we cut sin out of our hearts? How can we defeat the Prince of the Air?'

Smeaton's theme was familiar for anyone raised among Presbyterians – the moral turpitude of Scotland, the chaos of the times, the omnipresence of evil. It chimed well with the mood in the church – there were murmurs of agreement after every sentence.

'Satan walks in this land', Smeaton continued, raising his voice. 'We must seek him out. All those who serve the Lord must seek him out. We must seek out Satan and those who follow him. We must seek out blasphemers who reside among us in this corrupt country called Scotland.'

Scougall stole a quick look down at Chrissie. He knew she was more sceptical than him and gently poked fun at some of the more austere Presbyterian beliefs. He realised, as he looked at her, that he was no longer the blind believer of his youth. He could not help feeling they were observing an elaborate play. It was the first time he had felt this about a sermon. The minister was just a performer and the congregation his audience, lapping it up like thirsty dogs. Perhaps it was because he had been asked to play a role that he felt like an outsider in the Kirk. He knew Scotland was in a bad shape – a civil war was spluttering out, there had been long, bloody years of disagreement about religion and politics, and the trade of the nation was decayed since the revolution. There were evil men in the land – grasping, cruel men; he had personal experience of a few of them. But Scotland was surely not as bad as Smeaton described, with witch and warlock waiting round every corner. He was suddenly bored by the minister's pronouncements and laborious quotations from scripture and he wondered how long the sermon would go on for. He tried to focus his attention on the Kerrs in front of him, but his mind began to drift. At one point, he felt his head drop. He had dozed off and Chrissie had nudged him in the ribs. He hoped he hadn't missed anything important but the Kerrs were still in the same place with heads bowed in prayer. He looked behind and noticed that Umpherston, who had taken a pew right at the back, had slipped out of the Kirk, as he said he would. The minister continued to thunder against the sinners in Scotland and elsewhere. Scougall's mind drifted again on to other matters, such as his favourite golf holes, in particular the sixth at Musselburgh and the third at Leith Links, and then the soft miracle of Chrissie's breasts. He wondered if she was with child. He did not want to say anything to her but closed his eyes and prayed she was.

At last, after almost two hours, it was finished. The Kerrs had played their part ardently throughout, praying with vigour. Scougall, who was desperate to relieve himself, ran to the cover of some trees outside the kirkyard and, by the time he got back, the worshippers had begun to walk back to the city. Chrissie was waiting for him, chatting with Umpherston. 'I slipped out for a couple of pints, Davie. There's a good inn down there in Cramond. Fortunately, I missed most of the sermon!' he slurred, showing the signs of inebriation. 'They have a fine brew in Cramond!'

'It went on a bit long', replied Scougall in a whisper.

'You should have come with me, Mr Scougall. We could've talked about something more interesting', said Umpherston, smiling slyly.

'Your brother and sister-in-law did not miss you, Mr Umpherston?' Chrissie asked, innocently. Scougall knew he should be asking the questions.

Umpherston smiled. 'I better walk back with them. Ah, there's my niece, Beatrix. My brother's daughter. She's thick with Jane Montgomery. They go off every day to pray together. It's all a strange business, if you ask me.' Umpherston left then to join his family.

The walk back to Edinburgh was uneventful except for one incident. Jane and Beatrix, Umpherston's niece, disappeared into the woods together at the side of the road near Craigleith Quarry. Scougall thought about following them, although it would have been conspicuous. However, they reappeared after a few minutes, running to catch up with Mrs Kerr and Mary. He caught a dark look on Jane's face and a disgruntled shake of her head when Beatrix returned to her mother and father. When they reached the city, Scougall thought it had all been a waste of time.

After taking Chrissie back to their apartments, he met MacKenzie in the Periwig and described everything he could remember of the day over a bottle of wine. MacKenzie seemed satisfied enough with his spying.

'Thank Chrissie from me', he said. 'I have some news myself, Davie. I received a note from Kerr's neighbour Douglas today. He has remembered the name of the man he saw knocking on the door of Van Diemen's Land. He's an apothecary with premises in Gray's Wynd called Simon Fraser.'

A perturbed expression came over Scougall's face and he put his glass down on the table.

'What is it, Davie?' asked MacKenzie.

'Simon Fraser is the father of Alexander Fraser, sir', said Scougall.

'Alexander Fraser', repeated MacKenzie.

'Alexander Fraser is the student found guilty of blasphemy. Alexander Fraser will hang on the Gallowlee in a matter of days', said Scougall in a solemn whisper.

MacKenzie nodded. 'And Jacob Kerr sat on the Session that judged Fraser's case and passed it up to the Justiciary. Tomorrow I need to find out why Fraser's father was so eager to see Kerr.'

CHAPTER 9

The Testimony of an Apothecary

THE NEXT MORNING, MacKenzie received a note from Dalrymple telling him Kerr's funeral was planned for the following day and asking him about progress on the case. MacKenzie replied in a non-committal way and after breakfast made his way to Gray's Wynd on the south side of the High Street beyond the Tron Kirk. Simon Fraser's premises were about 20 yards down the wynd on the left.

MacKenzie entered the small shop, closing the door abruptly behind him to announce his arrival. It was a room full of bright colours and strange pungent odours. On the shelves were a myriad of bottles of all shapes and sizes with phials, boxes and instruments everywhere. MacKenzie's eye moved along the labels of a line of bottles on a shelf: almond oil, cannel, capers, figs, mace, saffron, orange peel, caraway seeds, verdigris, poppy seeds, hellebore root, opium. A figure emerged from a doorway behind the counter, a man of a similar age to MacKenzie with a pale forlorn face.

'Are you Simon Fraser?' asked MacKenzie.

'I am, sir. How might I help you', said Fraser with little enthusiasm.

'I'm investigating the killing in Van Diemen's Land', said MacKenzie and waited for a reaction.

Fraser shook his head and closed his eyes, summoning up the strength to answer. 'I'm sorry to hear of Jacob Kerr's death. It must be an awful shock for his family.'

'I've been told you were a visitor to the house recently?' asked MacKenzie.

Fraser looked shocked and staggered on his feet. For a moment MacKenzie thought he might collapse, but the apothecary supported himself on the counter and took deep breaths until he had recovered.

'Do you want something, Mr Fraser? Some wine or brandy to revive you?' asked MacKenzie.

Fraser shook his head. 'It will pass, sir. I am sorry. It's a trying time for me.'

'Your son?' asked MacKenzie sympathetically.

Fraser nodded. 'I wait on tenterhooks for news. I pray for a reprieve. I have used every ounce of influence I possess. There is still some hope I'm told. The King might intervene at the last moment. The Privy Council may commute the sentence to imprisonment.'

'It appears an unjust case, Mr Fraser. I hope the Council apply some reason to it.'

Fraser nodded. He raised himself and observed MacKenzie carefully.

'These are difficult days for you, Mr Fraser. But I must ask some questions. I've been appointed by the Advocate to investigate Kerr's death. What was your reason for visiting Van Diemen's Land?'

'As I said, I must use every last bit of interest. I knew Jacob Kerr. Not well, but we had done some business in the past. He sat on the Kirk Session. I asked him to intervene on behalf of Alexander, so the case would not be passed to the Justiciary. I told him it was only a drunken rant. Alexander meant none of it. I begged him.'

'Did he support your son's case?'

Fraser shrugged his shoulders. 'He said he would give the matter his close attention. He would listen carefully to everything that Alexander said when he was questioned by the Session. He would see that justice was done.'

'The Session sent the case to the Justiciary', stated MacKenzie.

'My effort was wasted, Mr MacKenzie.'

'Did you return to Van Diemen's Land after you heard the decision of the Session?'

Fraser was about to answer but drew back and was silent for a few moments. He looked MacKenzie firmly in the eyes and said, 'I have not been back there since, Mr MacKenzie. I knew that if I returned I could not contain my anger. It would do Alexander's cause no good. I need to control myself to make his case to others.'

'Is there any other family member or friend of Alexander's who was particularly angered?' asked MacKenzie.

'My wife is dead. My parents are dead. Only a few distant kinsmen live in the city who I have little time for. Alexander's friends have all turned against him and appeared as prosecution witnesses in court.' Fraser shook his head and sighed.

MacKenzie nodded solemnly. 'Thank you for your time. I'm sorry about your son. I hope common sense prevails and the boy is released. Good day, sir.'

MacKenzie walked back to Van Diemen's Land deep in thought. Had Kerr raised unwarranted hopes that he could block the case? Could Fraser have killed Kerr in a fit of revenge for not helping his son? Could he have entered the house and hidden somewhere or had he paid someone else to kill him? However, the slaying of Kerr would hardly help his son's case for reprieve and he appeared a genuinely devastated father.

MacKenzie was shown into the living chamber again by Jane. Mrs Kerr was in her usual place at the window, looking down on the courtyard. When she turned, MacKenzie saw that she was recovering: colour had returned to her cheeks and the expression of anxiety was gone from her face. Her black dress revealed an attractive, shapely figure. As she stood a few feet in front of him, he was overcome by a feeling he had not experienced for a long time. It was so surprising, he chuckled to himself. The feeling of sexual desire swept through him – desire for the woman before him, the relict of Jacob Kerr. The ache took his breath away. He was almost an old man, for God's sake!

Memories of his youthful days in Paris and Venice, when he had thought himself a lady's man and entertained a profusion of actresses, flashed through his mind. He smiled to himself. The birth of Geordie had obviously brought significant changes to his humour. For years since his wife's death, he had lived in a tunnel of self-absorption, afflicted by melancholic attacks interspersed with brief periods of forgetfulness. Now he was a doting grandfather, overjoyed by each smile of his grandson. But here was something else remarkable, as if life was returning to him again, and the feelings, long suppressed and dormant, were bubbling to the surface in the most unexpected of places – the living chamber of Van Diemen's Land during a murder investigation.

A voluptuous vision flashed through his mind, an erotic and absurd one, of taking Mrs Kerr in his arms and making love to her. He knew it was ridiculous. She was in the midst of the maelstrom caused by her husband's death. He could not act on the feeling. He would not act on it. But for a few moments, he was left speechless as the sensations flowed through him, enveloping him. There was still, perhaps, the possibility of some joy in this strange journey called life.

'Are you all right, Mr MacKenzie?' Mrs Kerr asked after a few moments, coming closer and staring up at him with a worried expression. 'You look distracted. Will I call you some wine?'

MacKenzie came back to himself and a wide smile spread across his face. 'I'm sorry, madam. Memories of long ago. Thank you for seeing me at this early hour.'

'Have you found out something?' She stood almost under him with her arms folded defensively across her chest. The thought of what he had to ask her curtailed his incipient desire.

'Again, I have difficult questions, madam. But I must ask them. Please sit down, Mrs Kerr. I believe I've made some progress in the case.'

She raised her eyebrows and a concerned expression spread across her face. He took a seat and she sat opposite him.

'As I've said already, I don't believe this house was robbed', he said frankly, waiting to observe the reaction on her face. She continued to wear the same look of apprehension.

'I don't believe your husband was killed by a thief', he said and waited again. There was no reaction. She sat stonily in front of him. 'Let me explain', he continued. 'The lock was broken from the inside and the kist was emptied to make it look like a robbery. The items inside dumped somewhere or hidden. And I found this concealed in your bed chamber.' He removed the knife from his pocket, opening the rag to show her. 'I believe this is the weapon used to kill your husband. It was under the floorboards beneath your bed.' He waited again to observe her reaction. She stared at the weapon in horror.

After a few moments she asked, 'What exactly are you saying, Mr MacKenzie? Are you are suggesting I was involved in killing my husband? You think I hid the knife there?' she asked, suddenly adopting an angry tone.

'I don't know who's responsible, yet, madam.'

She looked at him sharply. 'It's preposterous! Why would I kill him? It must be someone from outside', she said briskly. 'I know Agnes and Jane. I know my own daughter. They would never kill anything, nor would I, as a religious woman. If I did so, I would be bound for the agonies of Hell.'

'That is why I must ask more questions of you all. It's possible someone gained entry in another way', said MacKenzie.

She rose and returned to the window. She stood with her back on him and MacKenzie continued to question her from his seat. 'I want to know about the wounds on your daughter's arms. Why does Mary cut herself like that?'

Mrs Kerr did not answer at first. She put her hands on the window ledge and her head dropped. For a few moments she stood motionless in the same position, hardly moving, then suddenly turned and came back to her seat. She looked at MacKenzie forlornly, her anger gone. 'She's a delicate girl... a nervous girl. She's prone to... irrational fears. When she was young, she saw things in the house – she saw angels and spirits in her room. Sometimes she saw devils and demons and monsters. She began to cut herself. I do not know why it started. She believes Satan is tempting her to sin. She believes she can conquer Satan by cutting herself. She will conquer Satan with the help of prayer and through the guidance of the sisterhood.'

MacKenzie took out his pipe and tapped it on the arm of the chair, before continuing. 'I ask you again, madam. Did your husband mistreat any member of this household?'

There was silence. Then, at last she said, 'Not to my knowledge.'

MacKenzie stood up and let his mask of affability drop. Raising his voice, he pointed at her with his pipe. 'Tell me the truth, madam. Van Diemen's Land was no happy house. It was no pious idyll of prayer and worship. I've heard tell of terrible suffering behind these walls, suffering your husband was responsible for.'

She stared at him coldly, a hint of venom in her eyes. 'You assume wrongly, sir. There have been tears in this household, of course there have. I have shed tears myself. I have suffered. I have suffered… miscarriages. I will not deny there has been suffering but only that of men and women struggling to find the Lord.'

MacKenzie continued to glower down on her. 'I wish to speak to your daughter again, madam.'

'She's gone out early. She will concur in all I say.'

MacKenzie conquered his anger. He wondered who she was protecting. Was it Mary or one of her servants? Was she just blind to what had happened in the house? Or was she covering up for herself? 'I'll have a word with Agnes and then leave', he added, taking his hat.

In the hall, outside the living chamber, he was surprised to see Agnes coming up the stairs, breathlessly.

'I was coming down to see you, Agnes', he said.

She was flustered and short of breath and paused to gather herself. 'I was looking for you, sir.' She looked around cautiously to make sure no one was listening, checking the living room door was closed. 'I've found something, sir. I think it's important.' She removed a small, leather-bound book from her apron and handed it to him. 'I found it in Jane's room', she said. 'Thomas told me she kept it. He knew where she hid it.'

MacKenzie looked at the small volume. He could easily hold it in one hand.

'You must read it, sir', she continued, earnestly. 'It will tell you who killed Mr Kerr.'

MacKenzie raised his eyebrows in surprise.

'How do you know what it says, Agnes? I thought you could not read.'

'Thomas read some of it to me. He could not read it all, but he could read bits. The parts he read are…', her face darkened and she shook her head in disgust. 'Read it for yourself. You must decide, sir.'

MacKenzie opened the book and observed it was written in a tiny, neat script. He recognised the same hand that had annotated the volumes in Jane's room. Flicking through the pages, he read a few random sections. It was a diary of the kind often kept by religious enthusiasts, not an exact daily record of events, but rather a series of spiritual reflections. 'I'll take this back to my chambers to read, Agnes.'

She nodded. 'You'll find the answer you're looking for in there, sir.'

MacKenzie returned to Libberton's Wynd without hesitation. He asked his old servant Meg to light a fire in the study. Making himself comfortable in an armchair, he poured himself a whisky and took up the volume. His dog Macrae lay contentedly at his feet, pleased by the unexpected company.

CHAPTER 10

The Spiritual Exercises of Jane Montgomery

5 JUNE 1689: I BEGIN my exercises on this my first day in Van Diemen's Land. At last I am a woman in my own right, free to do as I wish, when not engaged with my chores, and provided my own chamber for the first time in my life. It is a blessing from God. Although a tiny room, I treasure the peace it offers me. It is a place where I can commune with the Lord.

10 June 1689: My master and mistress are accommodating, the house as clean and holy as I could wish. My master an elder in the Kirk, a revered merchant, held in high regard by all the godly within the community. I miss my mother with all my heart, but I am relieved to be away from my father's mockery. I grow close to Mary, the daughter of the house, who is a sad, troubled creature. She battles sin like me. We seek out the company of Helen Sim and her godly sisters more and more. I meet with my sisters every day and I savour their society. Agnes is not pleased to see I am favoured by Mary. I have heard Agnes is a creature polluted by sin.

12 June 1689: I cannot remember exactly the time and place the Lord first did me good in this world. I believe it was when I was still a tiny child, perhaps a bairn of three or

four years old, still hugging at my mother's apron strings. I remember asking her about the place called Heaven which I heard mentioned in the Kirk. I remember mother saying to me it was where I would be given fine clothes and everything would be brave and bonnie. I would dine on sumptuous food at the Table of the Lord with the righteous. I would want for nothing. I was delighted to hear this and desired more than anything to have assurance I would be one of those promised a place there. I learned from my earliest days that only a few of God's creatures would be saved at the end of the world, the rest bound for eternal torture in Hell. Since then I have hungered for the Lord. I have sought His feast of love as it was revealed to me as a child on my mother's lap. I now know I have expectation of eternal repose in Heaven with my mother and the angels in the presence of the Lord. Sadly I doubt if I will find my father there, he being an awful sinning creature.

16 June 1689: When I am engaged with Christ, all my sins are cast asunder. The brightness I see is like the sun bursting forth from clouds after rain. When I receive the sacrament, I am overcome with joy and weep for my eternal soul. Happiness washes through me like fresh running water. My spirit is cleansed of sin. Satan has no power over me and my predominant sin is diminished. It is like a feather, blown by the slightest breeze. I am at ease with myself and content in all things. I am not haunted by thoughts of unbelief.

21 June 1689: When I am at ease with myself, all is well in the world. I could not be a happier creature. Oh, a stake to be burnt at in the name of Jesus Christ! Even a gibbet, even the darkest prison, is nothing to me if Christ is with me! If Christ is beside me. I hunger for Him as a man desires food after a fast. If I am with Him, I can face anything in this

world of sin. Oh, how cheerfully could I embrace a burning stake, if I knew He was with me! I would not fear the flames, if I was with Him, if I had Him in my heart, if I was assured of His love.

26 June 1689: How wrong are those sceptics so prevalent during these days who claim religion is a melancholy thing. A carnal man or woman does not know joy until they commune with Christ, until they covenant themselves with the Lord and bind themselves to Him like two ropes spun together made indestructible in that bond. When I have assurance of His grace, I am like a vessel filled to the brim with happiness. All my doubts are taken from me. I am tempted no more to blaspheme or sin. The dreams that pollute and taint my nights are nothing and my days are full of light. My predominant fades to nothing. I think not upon myself. I am rid of myself. O the sweetness I see in that Holy Cross on which Christ Jesus was crucified and the great advantages attending His sacrifice! Then I believe I am saved from the beginning of time and will enjoy eternal bliss. My name is written in the book of life. I belong to God's holy elect. I will not be condemned to eternal torture like countless creatures wedded to sin.

3 July 1689: I often perform secret prayer in my chamber or in the kirkyard or in the fields beyond the city wall. At such times, I pour out my heart to the Lord. I engage myself to be His servant forever. I am covenanted with Him and assured of his love. Oh, what joy and contentment I feel! I am the happiest creature alive. I wish all other beings might know such rapture.

14 July 1689: Oh the sweet intercourse I get with Heaven in my chamber. A glorious night, a wondrous night, one I never

enjoyed the like of in all my life, spent wholly in prayer, down on my knees on the floorboards until the dawn. I slept not a wink all night, but I am not weary in the morning – rather, refreshed – as if I had deep slumber. My rapture is so intense, all else is nothing. The work I do for my master is nothing. The lives of my parents and brother are nothing. The lives of the worthy ministers of the Kirk are nothing. The lives of Mrs Kerr, Mary and Beatrix are nothing. Even the life of our beloved King, who hath saved this nation from the Papist menace, is nothing. All are nothing compared to my love of the Lord.

21 July 1689: It is from this day I mark my struggle with evil. I awake suddenly in the night. Something has roused me from sleep. Someone or something is in the room beside me. I hear breathing like the panting of a hound. I am terrified to see a figure in the darkness, looking down on me, standing motionless at my bedside. At first, I think the Devil has come for me, seeking me out for his coven. I am gravely shocked when I recognise the features of the creature in the half light. It is my master standing at my bed. He tells me in a whisper he must have me, he can contain himself no longer. He has desired me since he first saw me. I pull up the blanket and shake my head. He gets down on his knees and begins to pray in a whisper, beseeching the Lord to free him from the lust which plagues him day and night. He cannot cease thinking about me. He cannot stop watching me. He has prayed again and again for the Lord to cool his desire and turn his mind from me. But the Lord has not done so. Why has the Lord not assuaged his lust? Why has the Lord not intervened, Jane? He asks me desperately, putting his hand out to touch me. Such silence must sanction fornication between us, he says. I remain petrified in my bed.

When his prayer is done, he rises from his knees and looks down on me with an awful look in his eye. I tell him he must leave my chamber before he commits a grave sin, before he endangers his eternal soul. He stops for a moment and shuts his eyes. He shakes his head and ignores my pleas, unfastening his breeches, revealing himself aroused. I tell him again to be gone, that what he intends is sin, but he falls upon me, pulling the blanket away and trying to rip off my night dress. I fight against him with my fists, but he whispers that if I scream, I will be cast out of the household. I do not know what I should do. I do not want to return to my parents. I hate the stink of him and the weight pressing down on me. I am disgusted by him. I call out for him to cease. He stops his attempt, raises himself and strikes me across the face. Then hits me again, harder on the other cheek, calling me whore and jade and hussy and uttering blasphemies I cannot write. Then he continues his debauch of me. I am too scared to call out again. There is great pain inside me but it is done soon. He whispers to me that I am the Devil's creature who has led him astray. I am a witch who has bewitched him. He will pray for my immortal soul. He leaves the room without another word.

I do not sleep the rest of the night fearing his return. I place a chair against the door to block his entry. I recall my previous meetings with him since I came into the household, worrying I have encouraged him in some way. I wonder what kind of creature I am. Am I covenanted with God or a servant of the Devil? Is Jacob Kerr an emissary of the Devil or is he the Devil himself?

27 July 1689: Sin is part of me, like the thread woven into the cloth of my skirt. I can do nothing to unstitch it from the fabric of my being. I can do nothing but sin. My nature is to sin. I can go nowhere without sin. It is embedded within me

like precious stones fathomed in the earth. How can they be removed but through mining by the light of Christ?

4 August 1689: I am awake suddenly in the middle of the night. I do not know where I am. I think I am somewhere in the wide world. I find myself in a dark wood. He is looking down on me with lustful eyes. He is in the shape of a man, tall and strong. I bow down before him. I have come to this place with others who surround me in the darkness. I do not know who they are but I follow everything they do. It is the first time I have been to this place. I do not remember how I came here. There is fear in my heart, but also desire, intense desire. I know he is my Lord. I know I must worship him with every particle of my being. I must give everything of mine unto him. We are standing in a clearing in the woods. We walk around a fire in the darkness, hand in hand together. He stands in our midst like a statue. We do homage unto him as our lord. We sing unto him, praising his glory in a strange tongue. I do not understand the words that come from my own mouth. But I know that by them we praise his authority over us, his sovereignty over everything under Heaven and Hell. We stop singing and stand before him. I am shocked to see the others cast their garments onto the ground and dance naked under the light of the moon. I cast off my clothes also, copying their provocative movements. I am aware of his omniscience and his omnipotence. He is the lord of all he surveys. He is the Prince of the Air. He is the King of Kings. He is called Beelzebub by some. He is called Lucifer by others. He is called the Fiend or the Deceiver. He has many names in this land of Scotland. He is Antichrist. He is the Devil. He is Satan. We stand naked in the firelight waiting for him. We care nothing for the other world. The world of the city. We have no thought for the land in which we inhabit our days. Is it the real world or is it just a dream? Or is this world the real one?

When it is done, he disappears into the darkness as the first fingers of dawn touch the sky. We change our shapes. Feathers grow on our arms, fur on our bodies. We are transformed into cats and dogs and hares and badgers and birds and bats and other beasts. I change into a bird and fly home in the sky. Falling to earth, I find myself outside my door. I climb wearily the stairs to my chamber and, exhausted, fall into deep slumber. When I awake, I recall everything in an instant. I pray with all my heart it is just a dream. It must be a dream, I tell myself. How can it be real? How can I change my shape into a bird and fly in the sky? But why would I dream such things? Why are my dreams full of sin? Why would such evil enter my mind? Why would I participate in perversities I had no comprehension of before? As I lie in bed, I am relieved it is only a dream, but also appalled. The Devil has visited me, polluting me with depravity, just as my master has done. By this, he hopes to take me as his own. By entering my head when I am asleep and provoking such thoughts, he hopes to make me his. I am almost become a creature who has sold her soul to Satan.

5 August 1689: I tell something of my dream to Mary, although not everything. She agrees it is a warning. The next night she tells me she has had a similar dream. She was also taken to a dark wood where she saw a tall, black man. I tell her we will fight Satan together with prayer.

12 August 1689: I am cast down into a pit of despair. I am singular in my sinning. I am like no other creature in this wide world for sinning. Even the sins I have not yet committed in the eyes of the world have their seeds growing within my heart. Sin is like ivy upon the soul, infecting the roots of my being. My predominant seizes me when I am in the Kirk worshiping the Lord or when I am at secret prayer in my

chamber or in the fields or woods with my sisters. The Devil finds me. Satan tests me. I succumb and sin in my mind. I fear I am a worthless creature bound for Hell with no hope of redemption.

22 August 1689: Great is the darkness I suffer under when my mind is taken by sin. The cancer of disbelief grows within me. It is dreadful to confess my blasphemy. It is a habit I cannot be rid of. Under my breath in the house, even in the presence of my mistress, I curse and swear. Even on my knees when I am scrubbing the boards, I whisper vile words I dare not write on paper. They are foul words I have heard on my father's lips or on the street when taverns spew out their detritus. I am tempted more and more to shout out such obscenities when I am among my sisters or, God forbid, during a sermon in the Kirk. I am struck with a desire to proclaim everything the minister says is false, or worse, during Holy Communion, when I should be closest to God, I desire to blaspheme by saying: *There is no such thing as God*; *There is no such being as Christ*; *There is no such thing as the Holy Spirit*! When I come back to myself, the thought of shouting out these words freezes the marrow of my soul. I stand on a ledge at a great height, ready to fling myself into the flames of Hell. And in the night, only fitful and uneasy slumber awaits me, slumber haunted by dreams of Satan and his disciples, witches and warlocks when I give myself up to all manner of debauchery. Mary tells me she is afflicted by similar dreams. She fears we will both be suspected as witches and burned at the stake. It is as if this house is taken by Satan. Within its walls there is a battle for our souls.

5 September 1689: At times of deepest despair, I retire to the woods or fields outside the city walls for secret prayer. I go there alone and sometimes I go with Mary or Beatrix. It is

easier to seek out the Lord in these places. I beg Him to help
me turn from sin. I do not always find the Lord, but I pray
with all my heart for hours on end. I wander among the trees,
calling out to my saviour. I beseech him to protect me from
Satan and my master, as I wander the fields far beyond the
city. I find myself in a perfect wilderness, deep within the
cover of woods with no companion, under a canopy of trees,
far from any creature's sight or hearing. It is there I give in to
temptation. I call out and cry out aloud. I shout and scream.
I beat my fists against the trunks of trees. I rip clumps of grass
from the earth. I do not cease until I am weary with sinning,
until sin has had its fill of me. I return to the house and retire
to my chamber without sharing food with the family. Mary
comes to me and asks what ails me. I tell her I have a fever.
The family are glad I do not eat with them – plague is talked
about on the street; the people fearing it more than any other
thing, even Satan himself.

10 October 1689: As I reflect on how my master hath abused
me, there is wrought in me a new sin, one more vehement than
my predominant, which at first appals me, so contrary is it to
the laws of God. I begin to have a desire for it in the chamber
of my mind. Nothing pleases me more than the thought of it.
It is a terrible thought. It is the last thought on earth. It is the
thought of my own demise. It is the thought of my destruction
at my own hands. The fear I will not go to Heaven if I carry
out such a deed terrifies me. In my chamber at night I ponder
all manner of ways of self-murder, such as taking a knife to
my neck or wrist, adding poison to my cup, leaping from
the castle rock or high tenement, or throwing myself under
the horses of a coach. I am appalled I find pleasure in such
fictions. It is only through the intervention of the Lord I do
not carry them out. When I am close to the end of my tether,
when I am ready to act, He hears my prayers and comes to

me, calming the storm within my mind and easing me with a little sleep. The desire for self-destruction falls to nothing. In this way, I come to understand my life is a constant battle for my soul between the Lord and Satan. I share something of my struggles with Mary who tells me more of her own travails, although she does not tell me everything. I see she is afflicted by a bitter melancholy of the spirit.

30 October 1689: He comes to my chamber again, my master. This time with a knife in his hand. I am terrified. I know he is possessed by Satan. I know he has lost his soul to Satan. He is not one of the saved as he proclaims. He is bound for Hell. I fear for my life as he holds the knife to my neck, threatening to use it if I make a sound. Thankfully the vile deed is done quickly. I do not struggle although I hate myself for not fighting against him. He says I am good for not crying out. When he is done, he says he is sorry for it. The Devil keeps tempting him through me. He tells me I am infected by the Devil. He will pray more fervently for deliverance from lust. He will pray for my soul. I speak with Mary again this day. We are resolved we must do something to fight Satan in Van Diemen's Land.

12 November 1689: I reflect again upon my sinning nature. I think upon the many blasphemies I have uttered, within my mind or under my breath, and there arises within me a terrible corruption of self-conceit, as I sit in the Kirk listening to the minister, beside my master and Mary and Mrs Kerr. O self! That weary thing called self! I am plagued by myself, I say under my breath, as the minister preaches vehemently against sin. Oh, sinful self, I am weary of you! I can only see myself, even though I sit among this godly congregation, no others appear before my eyes. Even the Lord is invisible to me. Self blinds me to the Lord like a dazzling light. I think of

nothing but self. I am consumed by myself. I care nothing for my family. I care nothing for my mistress or Mary or Beatrix or my mother and brother. They are nothing unto me. They are as much consequence to me as the blades of grass I crush under my feet as I walk in the field or the tiny fishes gobbled by other creatures in that awful realm of water called the sea.

25 November 1689: I tell something of my doubts to Beatrix. She was brought up in a holy household in one of the sects who maintained the true faith under the rule of Antichrist before the glorious revolution allowed worship in God's house, rather than secretly in the fields. She has great care for me and shows much interest in me. One day she asks me to sit with her on a dyke at the side of a rig where we have retreated for prayer. Under the sun, I have some relief by unburdening myself of the woes afflicting me. I have spoken only a little of my distress to Mary. Beatrix appears concerned on my account. She asks me many questions, so I am almost overwhelmed by her interrogation, although I only answer some truthfully. I tell her of my battles with sin and the presence of Satan in my life. I do not mention my abuse by my master. Once she has heard me, she takes my hand in hers, holding it tightly. She tells me my case is not singular. She has suffered similar afflictions, although perhaps not as awful as mine, as have other sisters. She is afflicted also by doubts, one moment devout in the knowledge of the Lord with heart as light as a feather, the next cast down in deepest despair. Other sisters struggle likewise; some tempted by Satan day and night until they succumb, until they give up their lives to the prosecution of sin. Satan is always watching us, she tells me, waiting for the moment he can take us. He plagues us with musings, some ridiculous, others sins of the gravest nature. Thus, she goes on at length, sitting upon the dyke in

the sun. Her words are some medicine to me. I understand I am not alone in my sinning. There are others who suffer like me. She will speak again with me, she says. She will learn more about the nature of my sins, so that she may help me fight against them. I cannot tell her everything I have seen in my mind, or the vile words I have uttered, or the acts I have committed in my dreams or what my master has done to me. If I did so, she might think I am a witch and accuse me before the Session.

15 December 1689: I walk with Beatrix through the fields, talking of other things. She tells me about the day she was first covenanted with the Lord at a conventicle during the killing times. She expounds joyously on those days of suffering, which she remembers as the happiest in her life despite bloody persecution. I see Mary is not pleased I go off with Beatrix when I return to the house. She is quiet with me.

28 December 1689: I set aside as much time as I can for fasting and fighting my predominant sin. I dare not mention it to Beatrix or Mary, although it continues to have a hold over me, returning again and again. I know that Satan tempts me by it. Worse is in store for me; my predominant but a prelude to other abominations. And in their wake the most dreadful thought of all. The thought of unbelief and, finally, the blasphemy of self-murder, which chills me to the bone. But I desire it with a growing ache.

11 January 1690: I am told the sacrament is to be given in Lasswade Kirk, revered as a holy place where sisters often seek out the Lord, away from the bustle of the city. I have long desired to go there, hoping to find sweet communion with the Lord. Once I decide to go, my mind is calmed and my dreams inoffensive. I sleep contentedly all night long, untroubled by

my sinning nature. I am not tempted to blaspheme in private or public. I find myself a settled creature again, happy in God's care, untroubled by Satan, who is departed from my life – I dearly hope gone for good. I dare to think I might find some happiness as a creature promised everlasting life by the Lord. I avoid my master in the house and he does not trouble me.

20 January 1690: I am full of vigour in my work and strident in my prayers. I attend diligently to my chores. My mistress is pleased with everything I do. She praises me above Agnes, which troubles me a little. I see Agnes is jealous that I am singled out. I am happy in my tasks and work as hard as I can all day long. I anticipate with joy the journey to Lasswade. As a mark of affection, my mistress gives me a brooch, a gift which I treasure above all my possessions. I look upon it endlessly in my chamber after my labour is done. It is the most beautiful thing I ever beheld in my life. Agnes is not pleased when I show it to her. I believe she hates me for it. I am favoured over her, when I am a newcomer to the house. This, I believe, is how sinners regard those saved at the end of time, the small number chosen to enter the Lord's house, and bide with Him, at the end of days. I tell Mary I am bound for Lasswade. At first, she desires to go with me but she is taken by a fit of melancholy and cannot leave her room.

24 January 1690: I have another dreadful dream. I am back in the wood in the company of witches. We worship Satan lasciviously. I witness a multitude of abominations. I hear of killings planned for future days, contrived by witchcraft, including the slaying of bairns and other deeds of torture. The memory of them makes me shudder to the pith of my marrow when I recall them in the light of day.

30 January 1690: I am pleased to find the day a fine one; the sky a glorious blue over the city and not a cloud in sight. I take it as a good omen. I am strengthened by the thought of communion with the Lord and turn my thoughts from Satan and the master. I rise with the sun and without taking breakfast make my way to Lasswade with a cheery heart, leaving the city behind. I am allowed a day of leisure by my mistress. She is pleased to see me go, knowing I journey in the service of the Lord. I speak to no one and few speak to me on the road south. I enjoy the warm sun on my face. I do not feel alone. God is with me all the time. I feel as light as a feather and happy as a lark. The sun shines on me, warming my spirit. I am full of joy, my heart bursting and my soul thirsting for the Lord.

I come at last to the Kirk of Lasswade which makes my heart leap. I am surprised to see no crowd gathered in the kirkyard but it is still early in the morning. I am so eager to covenant with the Lord, I sped on the road without stopping to rest. I am so excited I can swallow no morsel of victual. Until the service begins, I decide to recreate myself by the banks of the river, a bonnie place, the water sparkling in the morning sunshine.

I make my way back to the churchyard thinking worship must begin soon, rejoicing in my heart and preparing to listen to the wise words of the minister. But when I reach the Kirk, all is quiet. I wonder where the worshippers are on such a day of fasting and humiliation. I wander among the tombstones in a state of confusion. At length I spy a beadle and ask him if it is the day of humiliation. He tells me terrible news. The fast was the day before. I have got the wrong day. I am too late, although I am sure Beatrix told me it was this day, which troubles me that she has been so careless. The news causes a jolt through my whole body, as if I am struck in the pit of my stomach by a fist. I can barely make reply to the beadle. I can hardly breathe. The news causes a sudden change in my condition. I burst forth in grief and sorrow; tears streaming down my face as I cry out in pain. The beadle is troubled, fearing, perhaps, I will accuse him of accosting me. My condition is changed in an instant, as though the happy hours before were worthless. The beadle tries to comfort me, telling me all is not lost, I will have other opportunities to covenant myself with the Lord. I should come back later in the year when the minister will return to preach here again. But there is nothing he can say to console me. I fall from a peak of happiness, where I stood only moments before, into a precipice of despair.

O then the enemy which I fear the most accosts me. The enemy of unbelief makes me entertain harsh thoughts of the Lord! I take the road home weeping when I came rejoicing. I am so distraught I take another path homewards. I cannot face the busy track to the city. The other way follows the course of the river. For a long time, I stand beside the water, staring at its currents and eddies, calling on the Lord to show me a path out of sin. But I walk in a tunnel of self, hardly aware of the world outside me. At length I come to a wood where I take refuge in the trees. I know not how long I am there, shedding tears and calling upon the Lord to aid me. I am reduced to a dreadful state, full of a black hatred for everything, even my beloved Christ Jesus. I cannot find Him or even a hint of the contentment I knew earlier in the day. I begin to utter profanities and blasphemies among the trees, vile words I have never spoken aloud before. I strike the bark of the trees with my fists until I draw blood. I tear out clods of earth and weeds which I throw about me, breaking the nails of my hands. I smash a plot of nettles with a stick, whipping the plants for their very existence. I fall down among them so I am stung on the bare flesh of my legs. I care not for pain. I care for nothing. *There is nothing!* I shout out loud.

There is no God! There is no Christ! There is no redemption! There is no Heaven or Hell! I shout these words loudly, again and again, in my distracted state.

It is then I feel it course through me. It comes from deep within the earth, a force rising through my legs into the very heart of my body. I have never felt such power within me before. It is my predominant, exultant, rising from the roots of Hell to flood my mind with sin. I am overwhelmed by it. I can oppose it no longer. I let myself be taken by it. I prostrate myself before Satan, just like in my dreams, giving myself up to him upon the floor of the woods and, once I start, I cannot stop. It is like a scab on my skin I must itch down to the bone.

At length, I come back to my senses in the world of men. I find myself lying in the fodder and muck, a despicable creature in a state of debauch. Satan has had his fill of me. I cry out in despair and thoughts of self-murder infect my mind. I am a pitiful, worthless creature. I think on whether I should throw myself into the river and be drowned. But a sound in the trees breaks my reverie. I see a figure walking towards me. It is a man, a young man. From a distance, I spy him. He does not see me, I think. My first thought is that it is Satan returning to have me again. But as I observe him meandering towards me, I realise he is not the Devil.

I am gravely shocked by the appearance of another creature and an awful thought takes hold of me. Has he heard the blasphemies and profanities uttered from my lips? Or worse, has he seen me engaged with sin, entangled with Satan on the floor of the woods? I cannot speak a word when, eventually, he stands over me, looking down on me as if he has come upon a sick animal. I look dumbly up at him. But it seems he has not heard my blasphemies, nor seen my deed, for he asks in a friendly manner what ails me. He heard me cry out and was concerned for me. He wanted to make sure I was not in danger from robbers or rogues who preyed on me. When I gather myself together, I can see he is a young gentleman, tall and slim with dark hair down to his shoulders. At first, I am too terrified to speak. He peers down on me to examine the cuts and grazes on my hands and arms and the tears on my face. I back off against the tree. He tells me not to be afraid. He wishes me no harm. He begins to talk calmly, trying, I think, to reassure me, telling me how he is spending a day in the country. He loves the woods and river, and desires always to be among nature, rather than in the city and the dismal world of men. He tells me what he has seen, the beasts manifold, including fish and herons and hares and deer, both does and stags. He would happily wander under the trees all day.

His words have a calming effect on me. He has not seen me engage with Satan. He looks on me without disgust and relief floods through me. I find my voice, speaking hoarsely at first. I tell him about my negligence regarding the date of communion and my bitter disappointment. He replies that I should rejoice. I am free to spend the rest of the day by the river, or in the woods, rather than in a Kirk listening to a dull sermon. I am ill-pleased by his words and show displeasure in my expression. I tell him the sermons of the ministry are nourishment for the soul. I will travel miles to hear a worthy preacher. He smiles at this, saying he has never liked sermons since he was a child. He says he will walk on the path home with me, if I will allow him, to make sure I proceed safely. He will walk all the way back to Edinburgh, if I wish, all the way to my master's door, to make sure I return safely. I am sorely tempted by his offer. But I sense sin rising within me and desire of self taking hold of me. Satan whispers to me that I should walk with this gentleman. I should talk to him and learn something about him. Is he not a fine-looking young man? Would he not be a perfect fellow to kiss and cuddle in the fields?

But I fight against my sinning nature. I tell him I must linger a little longer to visit a sister in Lasswade, a lie, but one that is necessary to avoid further sin. He bids me good day pleasantly, asking my name, which I give reluctantly. He does not press the point, which I am relieved at. It is strange because I am sad not to walk back with him. He says he will look out for me in the city as we are neighbours, he living in a garret not far from my master's house. He is recently finished at the college with time on his hands, until he decides upon a path in life. He takes his leave and wanders down the river in the direction of Dalkeith. I wait behind a tree, watching him progress along the river, stopping now and again to observe a creature or to touch a plant. He turns back to wave at me. I do not wave back, although I am taken by him. I am drawn to him, God help me. I pray he is not the agent of Satan.

It is a long, weary walk back to Edinburgh, along the road I skipped down a few hours before. When I reach the city, I go straight to my chamber. When it grows dark, Mary comes to my room and asks me about my day. I tell her everything except my engagement with sin. I tell her about the young man. She does not seem happy to hear about him. She says I should have nothing to do with him. He will only want me for one purpose – for fornication and then he will abandon me. She looks tired and weary but she will not share her sorrows with me.

6 February 1690: The master visits me again and debauches me. During the night, a plague of the heart afflicts me, a virulent disease of the senses, more dreadful than anything I have suffered before. My body shudders the whole night long. Only as the dawn approaches do I obtain a little relief from

the Lord who banishes the thoughts from my mind. I fall into a fitful sleep for an hour or two until I must rise for my duties.

12 February 1690: I am afflicted by lassitude of spirit with no desire to attend church on the Sabbath. I can hardly lift the Bible to read it in my chamber. I have no concentration to pray in secret. My mind flits like a moth about a candle. I have no thoughts of communion with the Lord and I forsake all my spiritual duties. I fixate on my engagement with sin and the gentleman. My predominant burns brightly within me. I cannot be rid of the thought of the gentleman, although I do not want to think upon him.

17 February 1690: In the blackness of night, I am never in greater hazard of my life. My predominant returns with spiteful force. It has taken sustenance from my defilement. It sweeps me away like a boat taken by a wave on the ocean, sending me spinning and reeling. I am tempted more and more. I battle with it constantly. I cannot banish it from my thoughts. My mind is in torment. I am haunted by illicit notions relentlessly, like a swarm of bees inside my head. My life is becoming insurmountable to me. Thoughts of self-destruction return with vigour.

In the middle of the night, I get out of bed and descend to the kitchen in my nightdress, proceeding with bare feet on the cold stones of the staircase with candle in hand. I stand in the kitchen in pitch blackness. I know not if I stand there for minutes or hours. At length, I take a knife from the press and hold it above my wrist, feeling the cold metal resting on my veins. The coldness of the blade calms me. I have a desire to end my life with all my heart. I love the thought of death. I will cut my veins and watch my blood spill onto the flagstones. I raise the blade to slash my wrist. At the last moment, the Lord comes to me. I do not ask Him to preserve me.

He tells me to put the knife aside. I return it to the press. I am just a stupid servant girl standing alone in the darkness. The candle has burned out. I return to my chamber in the pitch black, feeling my way with my toes on the stairs. I do not know if the Lord will preserve me next time.

19 February 1690: Mary comes to my room and opens her heart to me. She tells me things about the house. She tells me she has been abused by the master, her own father, for as long as she can remember. She has contrived to kill him often but rather than plunging a knife into him she turns it upon herself. I am deeply shocked by her confession. I comfort her and tell her what he has done to me. She is shocked by my confession. We pray together on the floor for deliverance from Satan.

24 February 1690: I see the gentleman walking down the High Street towards me, sauntering happily without a care in the world. My sin tells me to call out to him. I am drawn towards him like ore to lodestone. I think upon him with a selfish mind. I think on him rather than my Saviour Jesus Christ. A terrible thought comes into my mind, an absurd one, surely sprung from the Devil. What if one of my godly sisters, such as Beatrix or Mary, walked along the river with him rather than me, what if he asked one of them, while I refuse his company. Envy rises in my soul, sweeping all else asunder. I turn my head towards him to catch his eye, hoping he will see me, but I do not call out. He stops to speak to an old gentleman who greets him warmly and they go off together, no doubt to some coffee house or tavern. I hide behind a pillar at a shop front to observe him as he passes. He does not see me, which I am relieved at, but also sorry for. I do not have the courage to call out to him.

28 February 1690: I retire to my chamber for secret prayer, trying to rid myself of thoughts of the gentleman. After wrestling with my conscience for hours, I conclude he must be an emissary of the Devil. I must never speak with him again. But as soon as I tell myself this, I recall his features. Is it a false mask by which Satan hopes to ensnare me? Or is he Satan himself? I am washed by a wave of despair. However, a trifling thought disturbs me almost as much as the fear of the Lord – the notion that he will have no thought of marriage to the likes of me because I am far beneath him in the order of things, whereas Mary and Beatrix are daughters of merchants. He would want me for one thing, like the master. He would want me as receptacle of his sin, which would be death to me.

15 March 1690: The master returns to my chamber again. His debauch of me precipitates a battle within my mind. I can find oblivion only for a few seconds. I wake a thousand times from dreams of defilement. When at last the sun rises, I prostrate myself on the floor of my chamber, begging the Lord for relief from my misery. But He is silent. He does not come to me. Alas, my predominant has become my shadow. Satan beckons me to go with him. He asks me to walk along the river and lie with him on the soft moss of the woods. My mind is aflame. I desire it more and more each day and all of the night.

26 March 1690: I am conflicted in my heart about my master. I do not know whether he is a wretched sinner who should be pitied or an agent of the Devil who should be damned. I fear my predominant is born within me as my own liver, entwined with the fabric of my body and soul. I will never be free of it, whatever I do. I see no escape from my cage of sin. I am trapped like a poor beast. Although at other times,

when I am with my sisters in Christ, I obtain glimpses of grace.

4 April 1690: I share something of what has happened to me with Beatrix. She has become close to me, even closer than Mary. She says sharing my woes will help me be rid of such thoughts. But talking of it only encourages my mind in the persecution of sin, so that at night it is aflame with visions of fornication and no desire to quench it with the words of the Lord. Beatrix tells me Holy Communion is to be conducted in Largo. I have a great desire to attend to make up for my wasted journey to Lasswade. Mary will go with me but Mrs Kerr will not. I will seek out the Lord in an unfamiliar place, more easily to covenant myself with Him.

9 April 1690: We take a boat with our godly comrades. Half a dozen of us set sail from Leith with lightness in our hearts. As we embark the weather is fine and we look forward to hearing the minister, well-known for the sweetness of his words in the service of Christ. At first, we pass smoothly on our way over the water. But in an instant, all is changed.

A storm arises suddenly in the middle of the channel where the water is deepest. The sky turns dark like a bruise of heaven above the tiny boat and the wind gusts like a tempest. The waves swell around us, rocking the boat violently.

Mary is transported by fear, screaming frantically. She grips my hand, saying she is afraid to die. She cannot swim. The other sisters comfort her also. We all kneel together in the gunnels and pray to the Lord for safe passage. He hears our prayers. The storm is diminished and we reach our destination safely.

When we set foot in Fife, I feel the love of Christ coursing through my body in a stream. All my beloved sisters are exultant. We pray on the pier of Largo, huddled together.

Mary takes my hand and we thank the Lord, raising our voices to praise Him in song. I feel more assured than ever of the Lord's promise of everlasting life. I know in my heart it is written from the start of time. God loves me. God loves my soul. Nothing can alter the course of it. I have nothing to fear during all my days on this earth. All doubts are illusions. Satan will never take me when Christ is with me. Mary tells me she is also assured of God's grace. We are bonded together in his love.

The hours we spend in the land of Fife are of the greatest joy – indeed, they are the happiest hours I ever spent in the whole of my life in godly company with my sisters, my beloved sisters in Christ. For all the hours we spend in that blessed kingdom, I am not assaulted by one thought of sin. As the minister preaches in the Kirk of Largo, we feed off every word. When I receive communion in the Kirk, covenanting myself with the Lord, I cry out in joy as the Holy Spirit enters me. We spend the night together, all my sisters, praying in the fields of Fife, down in the very rigs of barley, in secret prayer as one, with no thought of self or sin, all night long unto the dawn; Mary beside me, holding my hand. I hear her prayers. She prays her father should be delivered from Satan so she will be free from his torment. It is a joyous night for us. We do not feel the cold as we are warmed by the love of God. We are together in Christ. But the Devil is always waiting to court us. He is never far away from us, even when we are in the arms of the Lord. He is always watching us. He is always waiting for an opportunity to tempt us.

12 April 1690: The pendulum swings back again. In my chamber, fearing the appearance of my master, I am plunged into a sea of troubles. My happy time in Fife is forgotten; all the pain I have experienced in my life before this night is nothing compared to the assaults I suffer as Satan begins

anew with me. Thoughts of self-murder, which had lurked under a stone like a snake, tempt me with a bitter smile. I see the dark features of Satan in my master's face and the suffocating oppression I will have to endure again at his hands. I am filled with dread he will debauch me again.

14 April 1690: This night is full of terrible thoughts all the way until dawn. I see a multitude of ways to commit self-murder, such as throwing myself off the crags of Arthur's Seat or drowning myself in the Nor Loch or taking rat poison from an apothecary's shop, and so forth, until I cannot count the number. When dawn breaks, I am dead in spirit and can hardly leave my room. I tell my mistress I have not the strength to carry out my duties. Instead, I slip out of the house and seek solitude in the woods by the Water of Leith, a place I have often sought the Lord and sometimes been rewarded with his grace.

I find a quiet spot where I take my piece of bread and cheese, sitting on the trunk of a fallen tree, gazing into the water and praying that God will give me strength to fight Satan with more vigour, so I might have relief from the turmoil engulfing my mind. I pray my master will no longer be afflicted by filthy lust. But I do not find the Lord. He does not come to me. Instead, I see another vision, shocking but appealing to my nature. It is the gentleman coming towards me along the path in the distance. At first, I do not think he sees me. He is lost in his own thoughts, speaking to himself under his breath. Then all of a sudden he is beside me, appearing from nowhere out of the trees. He is surprised to see me, and for a few moments, lost for words. I have had a little time to gather mine. I observe him more closely this time, establishing what kind of man he is. When he has gained his composure, he asks me if I am recovered after our meeting in Lasswade. I do not want to offend him. I have learned he is an apothecary's son, a man of some means in the world, although my sisters are uncertain about the extent of his fortune. For a short while, I am taken in by him, under his spell, as it were. I am content to talk with him. I fear he is witchcraft to my senses. We talk about nothing; all our words are idle chat. I find myself blethering like a gossip on the causeway, like women obsessed by the minute affairs of life who I despise. But I cannot help myself. I learn he has attended the college and hopes to become a doctor to cure the sick. I am pleased to hear he has such a worthy ambition. He asks me about my plans for the future. I tell him I seek only to serve the Lord. I aim for no higher place than the calling of maid. He asks me if I would ever travel beyond the realm of Scotland to see something of the world. I say I have a place promised me in a household in the north of England which I might take to obtain some knowledge of that southern kingdom. He says earnestly that he desires to go to a colony, perhaps as a doctor or in some other capacity. They need young men with skills to build a new world, he says. They will also require young women, if the colony is to prosper, so the settlement may be brought to fruition. He stares at me with his large eyes. I am quite taken in by them. I am quite taken in by him. I am surprised to discover his words kindle in me a desire to travel to the settlement he describes, a desire to travel wherever that place may be. To take his hand and follow him wherever he leads. It is a stupid thought, but one that bubbles up into my mind. I am shocked when he offers me his hand. It is a new thing for me to hold another creature's hand in affection. Little waves of pleasure pass through the whole fabric of my body. We rise from the trunk and, hand in hand, walk back towards the city. I am content with idle chatter and have little thought of anything else, until I spy a tinker approaching us. I drop his hand. I leave him at the city gate and walk back to the house fearful of my master's presence there.

19 April 1690: I meet Beatrix in Greyfriar's Kirkyard, the holy spot where the National Covenant was signed. We wander among the tombstones until she says something which stops me in my tracks. Out of nowhere, she asks me about the gentleman. I am flabbergasted to learn she knows anything about him, although I try to hide my surprise. She tells me things about him I do not know myself. He has the means to rent his own room in the city. He attended the college as a diligent student, although not a godly child. He is never seen in the Kirk on the Sabbath. I wonder why she is so interested in him. She talks on and on about him. I wonder if she has seen me in his company beside the river. I try not to show any interest in what she says. I wonder if she is a vixen playing a game, rather than the holy creature she pretends to be. Jealousy springs up within me, gripping me by the throat, so I can hardly speak. I must take my leave of her, claiming I am unwell. I cannot help feeling hatred towards her. It is the Devil's snare. I have a sudden revelation she is not the devout servant of Christ she would appear to be.

24 April 1690: I resort to the College Kirkyard before the sermon, a sweet retiring place where I have often found the Lord. I seek Him out again. I render myself unto Him, calling on Him to free me from misery. But He does not answer my calls. I hear only the sound of birds, chirping maddeningly as I wander among the tombstones. To my great surprise, into my sight through the gate comes the gentleman. For an instant, I fear he has been sent to beguile me. But my other self tells me I should speak with him in good faith. He addresses me in a friendly manner. He is pleased to see

me again and asks after my condition. I find myself talking with him, answering his questions and asking some of my own. I must know more about him than Beatrix. Forgetting why I took refuge in the kirkyard, I learn he has a sister who is 26 years old and hopes to marry a writer in the city. He is the grandson of a minister from the Western shires, well-connected with Presbyterian brethren there. I am glad to hear he has such godly heritage. He asks me if I will walk with him by the river of Leith one day. It is his favourite place in the world. We might take victuals together and go up to the hills and share a pleasant day. He knows many beautiful spots along the river and in the foothills of the Pentlands. I am sorry to confess I am tempted. I am pleased to be in his company. I find it easy to speak with him now I know him better and see he does not just sport with me. I am a bonnier creature than Mary with her fearful expression and Beatrix with her sauciness. I have heard folk say my countenance is a fair one. But such vanity means nothing to God, I tell myself, although I cannot help thinking it. I long to say I will go with him along the river. At last after much persuasion I resolve to go. I will walk with him one day soon. I desire it much. I desire it above all other things. We agree a place and time.

26 April 1690: I feel elation in my heart. Is he not a fine young man who will make a good husband? I tell myself he bids me well. Might he let God into his heart once we are married? We will pray together as a happily married couple, down on our knees beside our marriage bed. We will bring up a family in the bosom of the Lord and live life by His precepts. We might live a long life together contentedly. I imagine taking a ship to the other side of the world. We will help to establish a godly commonwealth far away from the sins of this realm, with a little house and garden and a brood of bairns. Thus, I have a glimmer of hope I might find some

happiness in this vale of tears. But just as my mind fixes on this pleasant prospect, my mood darkens. I fall into despair again, recalling what my master has done to me and what he may still do to me. I am like a rocking chair, shifting back and forth relentlessly. I cannot set myself at rest.

29 April 1690: I resort to the fields beyond the city in the middle of the night. Alone in the darkness, without a candle, I pray under the moon. I have done it oft times before. I beseech God to assuage my sin, quench it and give me peace. I stand in the rig in the moonlight of a cloudless night. I feel the cool clods of earth under my feet. It is no good. I do not find the Lord among the oats, though I prostrate myself before Him, though I give my soul to Him. I get down on my knees in the clart of the wet earth. It is there in the rigs, in the dark of the night, it rises into me again. I defile myself with thoughts of the gentleman burning in my mind. I can hardly breathe for the wanting of him. It is a long walk back to the city in the dark with no hope of God's love. At length, when I reach my chamber, old thoughts stampede into my mind like a herd of cattle seeking fodder. *There is no Christ. There is no Trinity. There is no Providence. There is no Redemption. There is no God. There is only Nothing.* I see the only way to be rid of such thoughts is by the act which makes me shudder to the pith of my bones. The thought of self-murder brings me some relief. I revel in it all night long, with visions of my own destruction filling my mind.

2 May 1690: I have more words with Mary about the master. I learn he has molested her since she was a girl. The mistress knows about it. The master beats the mistress when she begs him to stop. Mary has thought of turning a knife upon her own neck. I am shocked we share the same thought of self-murder. She takes some comfort from our joint pain.

She asks me what we are to do. She has thought of running away, but she does not know where she should go. I tell her we will fight Satan together. We will act to end our torment.

4 May 1690: I observe myself in the glass. I make sure I am presentable, my hair well-attended, my skirt clean and pressed. I am pleased with the vision in the mirror. A pretty maid, I would call myself, with bright eyes, full lips and dark brown hair. That is on the outside. On the inside, I do not know who I am. I do not know what I am.

I walk with the gentleman along the river. I am recovered in spirits after talking to Mary. I am not alone in my suffering. We will act together, I tell myself. Prayer will be our guide. Through prayer we will conquer Satan. I have seen nothing of Beatrix and my jealousy is diminished. I prepare my basket in the morning with bread, cheese and apples, simple fare. I will not return until the sun is almost set. I am happy as I make my way through the town. I am just a maid on her way to meet her beau. There can be nothing wrong with that, I tell myself. I see him waiting for me on the steps of the Tron Kirk. He greets me courteously and we walk down the High Street, chatting idly about nothing. Once we are out of the city we proceed along a path to the river of Leith. It is a fine day, the sun shining righteousness upon us. I feel God must be content with what I do, otherwise why would he not darken the day with clouds and rain?

The gentleman is affable, talking of what he has been doing since we last met, asking me questions about this and that, turning his head now and again to look at me. I am taken out of myself by him. I think little upon religion. I do not consider my maker or my immortal soul. I do not think of my master. They are not subjects for a day such as this. He tells me all he knows about places far away like the Caribbean and Indies. He has read books in the library of a friend and in the college.

He will lend me a copy of one in his possession, if I want to read it. I tell him I have no desire to read such a work. I have everything I need in the Bible. However, his enthusiasm fills me with excitement. I imagine myself leaving Scotland in a great ship and starting a new life beyond this benighted realm in a land where Satan has no power. And so, I will be free from the creature inhabiting Van Diemen's Land. I would be a happier thing, untroubled and not tempted by sin.

We walk under the green canopy of the overhanging trees, alive with birdsong, with only a few folk on the path to bid us good day. He enjoys imparting knowledge about the creatures of the river, telling me about birds and fishes and others I have not considered before, even the worms living underneath the earth that appeared a vile breed of beast to me before. I see now they are also part of God's creation. They have many uses I had no knowledge of, in cures and ointments. Beside the town of Currie, we sit on a rock overlooking the river. We eat our fare washed down with the water running at our feet, which we scoop up in our hands, but verily, it is the best fare I ever tasted, wholesome and delicious, the water cool and refreshing. We laugh as we eat, although I do not know why.

As we sit at our victuals, he suddenly raises a finger to my mouth to hush me. I think at first it is because I am babbling like a gossip. But he points out a hind and its young standing in a clearing among the trees, not far from where we sit – a lovely sight – before a sound in the woods startles the creature and she takes off into the undergrowth, followed by her offspring. I recall the words of Genesis and say out loud without thinking, 'A hind let loose. Naphtali is a hind let loose, he giveth goodly words.' But my recollection of the words of the Lord casts a shadow upon me. I wonder if my immortal soul is in danger. Do I court sin from taking pleasure with the gentleman? It is a shadow I wish I could cast off, but it is always with me, even when I forget myself; it waits around the next corner.

I think on the stag who has given the deer its young. The antlers remind me of Satan and I recall the awful weight of my master pressing down on me. The poor doe is a pure spirit defiled in the base currency of the world of sin. The gentleman takes my hand and leads me down the path. My mind still a rocking horse, shifting back and forth. Stopping by a bush, he plucks a white flower from it, and offers it to me. I take the bloom, feeling his fingers linger on mine, gently. Is it a sin to enjoy his touch? The Lord made man and woman to procreate. My mind conjures a future for us again. I will be his wife and the mother of his children. I forget the corruption in my mortal soul. I will conquer Satan who hath taken the heart of my master. But what of my other self? How can I account for that other girl when I am so happy? Would he think I am a blasphemer or, worse, a witch, and condemn me? But my doubts melt away. With his love might not that other self be sent packing? Might I not serve God as a good wife and mother? He is not like my father. He is not like my master. He is gentle and kind. He is an entirely different creature from them.

At length, the path winds away from the river up towards the hills, a wild place I have never been before. As we climb the slopes of grass, I look back on the blue firth and the land fading to grey. Even sin, the dreadful spawn of the Devil, is a paltry thing up here among the clouds, with only as much power as the midges swarming in the air around us which I swat away with ease. We enter another wood, high in the hills, a secluded copse far from all other creatures with not a soul in sight. The world is reduced to us alone and we rest in a little clearing, he sitting beside me on the ground, close to me – too close I fear, but I say nothing. I like him there, my body tingling with his leg touching mine.

I feel as if something is about to happen and, sure enough, he kisses my cheek without asking permission. I recoil from his kiss with memories of my master entering my mind and for a few minutes I say nothing. But he continues to chat away, telling me silly things, that I am a pretty maid, as pretty as any in the whole of Scotland and that I am as precious to him as gem stones. The thought of my master fades. I am pleased to hear such trifles, although I know it is vanity. I observe I make him stand under his breeches, which, God forgive me, I am pleased to see, although it is a sin for me to look there. But once I have this thought, I recall my dreams of Satan and his coven of witches. I recall the horrible visage of my master on top of me and I rise suddenly to my feet. He asks what is wrong, if he has offended me. He sees my mood turns on a sixpence. I say I must return to the city. The memories of abomination have shifted my mood. I am tarnished. But he just smiles and holds out his hand. I take it and he leads me down the path towards the river without another word spoken between us. I am troubled for a few moments with thoughts of loathsomeness, but the feeling passes. We walk along the path hand in hand in the gloaming, my despair conquered for a while.

7 May 1690: Thomas seeks me out. He tells me he has been beaten by the master again. I am teaching him his letters and he is an able pupil. He shows me the marks on his back where the master has whipped him with his belt. He cries as he tells me this. He tells me Agnes says she will kill the master the next time he is beaten.

9 May 1690: There is an occurrence which afflicts me like a blow from a hammer. I am asked by my mistress to take a message to her cousin in the West Bow. As I turn down the steep slope at the Bowhead, I catch sight of the gentleman.

He is standing beside the low wall on the Castle Hill, talking to a woman in a cloak. At first, I think it is nothing, believing she is an old crone or perhaps his sister. I am about to raise my hand in greeting when the woman turns and I am shocked to see Beatrix Umpherston with a lascivious smile on her face, like a strumpet from a bawdy house. I move off into the crowd, unable to speak, anger burning in my heart like a fire. I deliver the note but I am in no mood to linger, my jealousy bubbling inside me like broth in a pot.

Much later, I join my sisters to pray in the orchard at the back of the college. Beatrix is among them but I can hardly look her in the face. She takes only a moment to complete her prayers before telling me of her meeting with the gentleman. He is known to her father, she tells me. He recognised her, stopping her on the street. He is a clever man who has passed through the college, although prone to the bottle like all students. I ask her shrewdly, I cannot help my tone, that if he is such dangerous company, why does she speak with him. She smiles, saying she believes he has money in his kist, giving me a sly wink. He will make a girl a sweet bedfellow, I am shocked to hear her say, as if she has designs on him herself. Jealousy rises within me and, God forgive me, I wish her struck dead. I dare not say to her I have spent time in his company. I have a sudden glimpse of my entanglement in a web of sin and realise I should devote myself to Christ rather than think about the gentleman. But I also see my godly sister is not as holy as she would appear. I believe there is more than a little of the vixen in her.

12 May 1690: I cannot sleep. It is not disbelief that impedes my rest – rather, desire for the gentleman. I try to forget the stupid strumpet Beatrix and recall him, again and again. I court silly hopes of becoming his wife and escaping my

master, alongside a terrible fear that if he should go with another woman I would fall into a darker chasm, one from which I would never escape but through self-murder. In the darkest point of the night, a terrible thought comes to me, one that makes me shudder to the pith of my bones. It is the thought that I would slay her if I had to; if I thought she would take him from me, I would do it without hesitation. I would push her head under water and hold it down until she ceased struggling. How can one of God's chosen think of such an act? Would I not be condemned to eternal damnation? And again, I fall into a dark pit. In my slumber I am presented to Satan. In my dream, I contrive with other witches to be rid of Beatrix. We manufacture a doll in her likeness which we pierce with bodkins. I dream of destroying my master by similar contrivance. When I wake, I know not what I should do with myself.

18 May 1690: I am surprised to have a visitor in Van Diemen's Land. I am perturbed to see her at first, recalling my dream when I contrived her murder by witchcraft. Beatrix has news which she must unburden herself of. Dreadful news that makes me shudder. The power of Satan increases within the realm, she says. Witches are in the air across the land with cases taken to the Privy Council and all manner of debauchery and vice prevalent, despite the admonitions of the ministers. I observe she revels in it, as if the thought of so much sin gives her pleasure. This town is full of blasphemers and Sadducees and fornicators, she warns.

Suddenly she takes my hand and pulls me down onto the floor beside her. On the boards we pray fervently for our immortal souls. I recall my blasphemous utterances in fields and woods. I recall the words inside my head, the blasphemies, corruptions and monstrous statements I cannot cease making. I think of my walk with the gentleman and my dream when I planned to murder the sister kneeling beside me, her hand in mine, and how I contrived to end the life of my master by witchcraft. When she is gone, my desire for death returns.

25 May 1690: I cannot stop myself. I am drawn to the gentleman as I am to the service of Christ. I will see him once more. I will tell him what we do is sin. I know he will not marry me. I am a maid with no tocher. I will not give myself to him for his pleasure, like a tavern lass or whore. It would be death to my soul. And what if he discovers my maidenhood is taken by Satan?

26 May 1690: We walk along the river again. I find myself becalmed in his presence, the anguish in my soul dissipating when I take his hand. We walk in the shadows of tall trees. The warm breeze is balm to my soul. I wish the moment never ended. I think it may be like the bliss promised at the end of time, but I banish the thought as foolish blasphemy. We reach the patch of wood high in the hills where we went before. It is a place captive in my memory, where love was revealed to me. As we rest on the trunk of a fallen tree, he places his hand on my waist and tries to kiss me again. But I blurt out angrily he only seeks me for sport, desiring to have me as a whore and other stupid things – I know not where my sudden rage comes from. I even declare I saw him on the street with Beatrix, a good for nothing strumpet. But he just laughs at my outburst and tells me it is nonsense – has he not asked me to go with him to the Indies? I should go as his wife, not his whore. I am calmed and my anger, which rose so violently, is spent. He kisses my hand gently. We walk back arm in arm in the gloaming. I am content for a while, holding his hand. We part at the West Port, promising to see each other again, although I had left a few hours before adamant

I would never meet with him again. When I return to my master's house, I pass straight to my chamber and fall into a slumber unspoiled by dreams, my mind empty like a deep ocean.

28 May 1690: I am undone by sin! I am overwhelmed by sin! I am assaulted by sin! I am crushed by sin! I am a tiny pebble under the vast weight of Satan. My mind is blown by storms and my body sent a-shuddering. I can find no escape anywhere. I have been stung by Satan. He has poisoned me unto death, the great Deceiver! I am his creature entirely; my hopes of redemption departed. I am bound for the flames of Hell to burn for eternity. I know not if I will ever find my way back to Christ. I am not one of God's chosen. I am just the plaything of the Devil! I hear news that a blasphemer is taken to the Tolbooth. At first it brings me joy. The magistracy continues to purify the nation by destroying the power of the Prince of the Air. It will help my own struggle with sin. What is more, I will soon be a married woman. I will soon be the wife of a doctor. I will soon be on the other side of the earth. I will leave Van Diemen's Land behind forever. When I am in congress with a sister in a field, I learn the name of the accused. I almost fall dead when the words come from her lips. It is like a thunderclap to me. It blows me widdershins. The name I hear from her lips is that of the gentleman I have sinned with in the hills. I recall I have heard him voice certain irreligious views. I thought him just teasing me. I never heard him blaspheme. He said he had doubts, but what Christian can claim they do not. I learn he has been questioned already by the Session, my master attending, and is held in the Tolbooth as a blasphemer, awaiting trial. I hear the story repeated later by Beatrix. She says nothing of speaking to him on the street and I say nothing of knowing him. We both understand we could be condemned as concurrent in

his blasphemies. I tremble on hearing this news; my peace of mind gone in an instant. I see I am truly a pathetic thing. My original suspicions proved right: the gentleman is Satan's agent sent to gather me unto his fold. What terrifies me most, striking me cold with fear to the threads of my heart, is the thought he will accuse me of complicity in his crimes; he will accuse me before the godly community. I am swept with shame. He will tell everyone he has seen my defilement. What is worse, he will accuse me as blasphemer. But, I tell myself, he does not know I have had such thoughts. Nonetheless, I have spoken them aloud in Van Diemen's Land. Have I been overheard by Agnes, who hates me, or a sister when I was distracted or by Beatrix? Have Mary or Mrs Kerr heard me blaspheme and betrayed me?

29 May 1690: I live in a constant fear of arrest. I cannot stop shaking, even when I sit before a roaring fire. I cannot eat a morsel. I vomit constantly. I cannot sleep a wink at night. I cannot find the Lord anywhere. He is gone from me for good. My beloved Christ is gone from me. He is silent when I call out to Him. I can find Him nowhere, though I seek Him constantly. I beg him on my knees to return to me. I hear my master tell my mistress how the Session does good work rooting out blasphemers in this realm.

30 May 1690: My mind burns with pain. I cannot quench the agony with the pure water of the Lord. As I take up my Bible, my hands shake, and I must lay it aside. I cannot read the words which are manna to me. I can find no ease in the words of God, although I seek it in prayer constantly. The Lord does not answer me. He is disgusted with me as vile sinner. He is done with me. I dare not visit the Kirk to hear a sermon. I will surely damn myself with my own words, calling out before the congregation that I am a

blasphemer's whore! I will surely utter blasphemies such as these: *There is no God, there is no Trinity, there is no Redemption*!

1 June 1690: I am come towards the end of my tether. I cannot last much longer in this life. The Devil is taking all of me, feasting on the dregs of my rotten core. Each night he returns to me. Each night he comes for me! He tempts me with all manner of debauchery. I present him with everything I have between the crown of my head and the soles of my feet. I render all unto him. I am marked by him as his own.

2 June 1690: I know my road leads to only one destination, predetermined from the start of time. I am not one of the chosen, but one of a million sinners born to endless torture in the eons of time. I fall into the deepest pit of despair. I fall into my old ways of thought. I cannot be rid of myself. I am tempted to self-murder more fiercely than ever before. It comes with a ferocity I cannot oppose, my mind plagued by manifold plans to achieve it, the desire coursing through my arms and down into my hands and fingers. I know not if the Lord will preserve me this time. By the act of death, I will be relieved from the pain of life, I tell myself.

3 June 1690: In the middle of the night I climb up to the garret, wearing only my nightdress. I climb out of the window onto the ledge above the courtyard. I stand beneath the stars, my hair blowing in the cold wind, the town far beneath me. The sky is cloudless, a million stars looking down on me, condemning me as inveterate sinner. I stand for a long time, thinking to cast myself onto the courtyard below. I will drop to a certain death. All the bones of my body will be smashed to little pieces. I will be found on the cobbles the next morning. The thought is a throb of desire

driving through me, although I know it is a grave sin to take my life and I will surely plunge straight into the flames of Hell. Surely they are preferable to this pain.

I do not jump to my death! God be praised! I do not jump! I stand on the ledge under the stars, peering down into the darkness. I do not jump. I want to jump. I want to as much as I have desired anything in my whole life. I stand with the wind on my face for I know not how long. And finally, the Holy Spirit enters me. The Lord returns to me, casting my legs like lead on the ledge. I cannot move when my mind tells me to jump. I cannot leap to my demise. The Lord takes command of me. He has taken my body and soul. As dawn breaks, I find myself becalmed, although still high on the ledge. The passion of my torment is dissipated. When I acknowledge God is within me, I find I can move my legs again. I climb back in through the window. I am resolved on what I must do. God has saved me for a purpose. I know I must slay Antichrist. I return to my chamber and fall fast asleep.

4 June 1690: I am recovered in spirits. I thank God for it. I get down on my knees in my chamber and pray, thanking Him for preserving me. I know it is for a purpose. I must fight Satan. I try not to think about the gentleman. I am visited again by my master. I despise him. I know he is the pathetic plaything of Satan. I know he is bound for Hell. He will be there soon enough. I will have my revenge on him soon enough.

5 June 1690: I am not sought out by the Session. I am not visited by any elder or minister. I am not accused by my sisters. Instead, a few sisters call on me to determine my condition. I am not mentioned at the trial of the gentleman. I listen on the street when I venture abroad. But each time I hear a knock on the door I fear they have come for me.

6 June 1690: I return to the comradeship of my sisters. I go to secret prayer again in the fields, which settles my spirits further. I talk with Mary every day for hours. We resolve to be sisters in blood. We share everything with each other and form a plan of prayer. I see nothing of Beatrix and wonder what is become of her. Some say she has left the city to hear a minister in the west where she has family.

7 June 1690: I am on my knees scrubbing out the hearth, when God allows me a glimpse of grace. A fleck of joy returns to me. I go back to the Kirk on the Sabbath to seek sustenance in the words of the Lord. I find deliverance from my travails. At night, my predominant is conquered. I think less and less upon the gentleman. It begins to feel like it was a dream. I wonder if it was true or all imagined fancy?

8 June 1690: I watch from deep in the crowd on the High Street as the gentleman is led out of the Tolbooth. I am startled by the change in his appearance. He is like a skeleton, death-like in his thinness, the sackcloth hanging off him, his young flesh decayed. He is no more a gentleman, more like a wretch or beggar on the street. He stumbles on the causeway, unable to walk in a straight line, as the crowd engulfs him in screams of hatred. Some call out against him as vile blasphemer. From far back, I pretend to shout with them, although I cannot. There are tears on my cheeks. Then out of the corner of my eye I observe Satan lurking in the shadows beside a pillar, watching me. I see the face of the Devil. It is the face of Satan. It is the face of my master. It is my master smirking at me lasciviously. I know my master is Satan. He has contrived the death of the gentleman.

The gentleman stands at the door of the Kirk, swaying like a reed in the wind. He enters the church and the moment is gone. I sit with my sisters at the back, barely able to see him on the stool at the front. He is a poor creature festered by sin, wasted by Satan. He is no longer a gentleman. He is no longer a young doctor hoping to sail around the wide world. He is a vile sinner, polluted with sin. But is God not bountiful? Will He not forgive our sins? Will He not forgive any sin? He will surely forgive me the sin of slaying Satan. The minister preaches with great vehemence, telling us the time we live through is like no other in the history of man. We are close to the end of days. If we do not repent, we will fall into Hell. God tests us. Satan tempts us. Thus is the battle fought during the last days of mankind. Never was a battle waged so fiercely across the land from east to west, north to south. Never was Scotland so afflicted by sin. Never has sin been so plentiful. Sin is the resin of the times. Sin is exuded everywhere, revealing evil in all its manifestations: fornication, Sabbath breaking, profanity, witchcraft, blasphemy. All of which must be punished by the magistracy. All of which must be punished by death.

Never has Satan had such truck with us. Never has the Devil been so much amongst us. Never has he been so close to us. He is the neighbour in our house. He sits in our privy chamber, a breath away. He is our mother and father; he is our brother and sister; he is our master and servant. He lies with his head on our pillow as we sleep. Never has there been such profanity, abomination, drunkenness, fornication done before the Lord. We must bow down before Him and repent our sins or He will have vengeance upon us.

Mary takes my hand as the minister thunders. I turn to her and she nods to me. We will fight Satan together. I bow my head. I close my eyes. I pray to God with all by heart. I thrust thoughts of the gentleman from my mind. I must be done with him for ever. The battle inside me is fierce, but it can be won with the grace of the Lord. I pray with all my heart, surrounded by my sisters, singing the holy psalms despised by Satan. They cannot know how much I am tempted by the Prince of the Air. They cannot know how much I have sinned in my mind and the abominations I have committed in my dreams. I pray with all my heart, until tears gush from my eyes and pour down my cheeks. I beg forgiveness for all my transgressions. I beg forgiveness for one final transgression. Praise be to God, I do not call out! I do not call out! I do not blaspheme before them! I have no desire to do it. I see my sin is just selfish folly, nothing more. The pressure on my temples eases. The storm passes from my mind. My predominant is vanquished! I pray that in his death, in the death of this blasphemer, I will find ease. By his death, the nation will find perfection. I rejoice in the vile blasphemer's destruction. The minister calls for him to be slain so we may be saved. In his demise, Satan is weakened. He tempted me, this servant of Satan. The monster employing me in his house has polluted me. But he will not have my soul! I have won the battle with sin. I will be forgiven at the end of days. I am a creature renewed. In his death, I will be saved. In his death, Scotland is saved. Oh, if He is with me, I will face anything, even the gibbet. If Christ is with me, I will face anything! If Christ is with me, I may do anything!

CHAPTER 11

Further Revelations

MACKENZIE HAD NOT touched his whisky, so engrossed was he in Jane's book. After he had finished reading, he sat for a long while deep in thought, gazing into the fire. Finally, he took up his glass and poured all the spirit down his throat, closing his eyes and waiting for the familiar burn in his gullet. He went to his desk and wrote to Scougall at his office asking to meet him urgently.

Twenty minutes later, they sat together in the Periwig; Scougall looking particularly fretful. He was busy preparing a bond for Mrs Hair and the summons was another unwanted distraction. But MacKenzie spoke with such seriousness that Scougall lost his appetite for arguing with him.

'I want your opinion about something, Davie', MacKenzie said, handing the small book to him.

Scougall read the first page, looking up, perplexed.

'Take it away and read it, carefully', commanded MacKenzie. 'It's an account of the last year by Jane Montgomery, the maid in Van Diemen's Land. I want to know what you make of it.'

Scougall nodded. 'I'll read it this evening, sir. I must finish something in the office first.'

'Come to Libberton's Wynd when you've read it, Davie', replied MacKenzie. 'Whatever the hour; it doesn't matter how late. I'll be waiting for you in my study.'

It was not Jane who answered the door when MacKenzie returned to Van Diemen's Land but Agnes, with an expectant look on her face. She must have been waiting for him. 'Then you've read it, sir. You've come back to arrest her?'

'I need to speak with her, Agnes. And to you, also.'

Agnes looked disgruntled. 'She's in the laundry, sir.'

MacKenzie moved in front of her, blocking her way. 'In the book, Jane says Thomas told her you said you would kill Kerr if he belted him again.'

She nodded. 'I may have blurted out something like that, sir. But I did not mean it. It was her, Mr MacKenzie.'

MacKenzie eyed her closely and left her in the hall. Descending to the kitchen, he went to the laundry door. Jane was ironing inside. She looked up at him fearfully. She was wearing no bonnet, her long black hair reaching all the way down her back.

'She should not have given it to you. It was my private thing. My most private thing. It was for me and God only.'

MacKenzie moved towards her. 'Why did you keep it, Jane?' he asked.

She put the iron down. 'It's a record of my suffering, sir; a record of my striving for a good life; a record of my battles with Satan. Many of the sisters keep spiritual diaries. Agnes had no right to take it! I want it back, sir. It's mine.'

'I will return it to you, Jane. But I must keep it for now. Is everything you write in it true?'

She did not answer immediately but turned her head to stare at the wall. She looked lost for a few moments. Finally, she spoke. 'It describes how I felt at the time, sir. I have struggled with myself. I wrote down the truth as it appeared to me. I only seek to serve the Lord. I only want to fight Satan. I strive to be a good Christian. I do not want to sin, sir.'

'What about the pages where you record your treatment by Kerr?' he asked tentatively.

She looked down tearfully. 'They are true, sir.' She turned to him, looking forlorn. 'That is the truth, sir. I swear in the

Lord's name. I could not make up such vileness. Why would I make up such vileness?'

'Why did you not tell me when I asked you before?' he asked, sympathetically.

'I could not… I thought it would destroy Mary and Mrs Kerr.'

'Kerr raped you?' asked MacKenzie.

Her head dropped and she began to sob.

'When did it first happen?'

'A few weeks after I started here, just as I describe in the book.'

'Did it continue since then?'

'I lived in fear of it every night I slept in this house. It happened every few weeks.'

'You say Mary was abused also', said MacKenzie.

'She suffered terribly over many years… years and years. You have not seen her when she is troubled. She is like a terrified animal, screaming against each second of existence. That is what Satan brought her to through her own father… that is how evil Satan is… she's been tempted by self-murder just as I have, as you will know from my diary. I have often been enticed by it. I have almost carried it out. She is the same. Each time she cuts herself she thinks of turning the knife on her neck. But the Lord has preserved her. Thank God.'

MacKenzie stood motionless for a few moments, staring intently at her. 'I'm sorry you've suffered such a master, Jane. I am disgusted a man should abuse you like that.' He edged closer and continued to speak softly to her. 'Did you kill your master, Jane? Did you end your torture by stabbing him through there in the kitchen? You can tell me now, my dear.'

She shook her head.

'Did you and Mary do it together?'

Again, she shook her head.

'Did you contrive to kill him with the help of your friend Beatrix?'

She shook her head.

'Or with the gentleman you mention in your book?'

'How could he help me, sir? He is in the Tolbooth awaiting execution.' She looked up at MacKenzie and shook her head vehemently. 'I swear I did not, sir. The book says nothing like that. I sought to fight the master with prayer. The Bible says thou shalt not kill. I could never disobey that commandment. I would only ever fight Satan with prayer – not with a blade!'

MacKenzie took his notebook from his pocket and read a few passages from her exercises: 'I tell her we will fight Satan together. We will act to end our torment... I speak with Mary again this day. We are resolved we must do something to fight Satan in Van Diemen's Land... I despise him. I know he is the pathetic plaything of Satan. I know he is bound for Hell. He will be there soon enough. I will have my revenge on him soon enough... I talk with Mary every day for hours. We resolve to be sisters in blood.' MacKenzie emphasised the last word and waited for a few moments. 'What you say suggests you planned to kill him. That's the impression I got from reading it from beginning to end. It's highly suggestive that you did more than pray for your freedom. It suggests you and Mary planned to kill him. And then he was found in a pool of blood in the kitchen!' he said, finally raising his voice.

Jane shook her head. 'I thought of killing him in my mind a thousand times. I dreamed of it, using witchcraft. But there is a difference between the thought and the deed itself. I have a motive, but so does Agnes, God forgive me.'

'Tell me why Agnes would kill him.'

'She was jealous of me and hated me.'

'Why would that make her want to kill him?' asked MacKenzie.

She looked at him, defiantly. 'Because once I came into this house, he showed no interest in her!'

MacKenzie shook his head in disgust. 'He abused Agnes too?'

'He visited her bed long before I came to Van Diemen's Land. Mary told me. Thomas is the master's bairn.'

MacKenzie thought of an onion again, the outer layers being peeled away. He knew he was getting closer to the kernel of truth. 'Kerr did not recognise the boy as his own?' he asked.

'He could not, sir. He could not do so without disgrace, he being an elder and sitting on the Session.'

'So, it was kept quiet?'

'Yes, sir. But Agnes admitted it herself, not long after I came into the house. She said she and Thomas would be favoured as Thomas was the master's bairn. I was not to get above myself or I would find myself out on the street. She had the master's ear, she claimed.'

'So you are saying she killed Kerr because she was jealous of you?'

She shook her head, looking confused. 'No, sir. The master beat Thomas severely. She could not take it anymore. She killed him for that reason. But she sought to blame it on me.'

'Does Mrs Kerr know you were debauched by her husband?'

'Mrs Kerr knows about Mary and about me', she replied vacantly.

MacKenzie stopped to think for a few moments. Taking his pipe from his pocket, he stuck it in his mouth and, without lighting it, sucked on it, before continuing. 'The young gentleman Alexander Fraser – the one found guilty of blasphemy – is what you say about him true? You walked with him in the hills? He promised to marry you? Is that fancy or truth, Jane?'

She looked desolate as she replied. 'I swear it is true, sir. I swear he asked me to be his wife. But he was condemned by the Session.'

'Did Kerr know Alexander's father?'

She turned pale and her head dropped. 'I do not know. But the master was on the Session that sent the case to the Justiciary.'

'Did you ever see Simon Fraser in this house?'

'I do not know what he looks like. The gentleman never crossed the threshold of Van Diemen's Land.'

'You wrote that you flew in the air to a coven where you worshiped Satan and contrived to kill by witchcraft', said MacKenzie.

'It was a dream or vision. The Devil visited my mind to trick me. I was taken to his world in the night. Satan was trying to control me', she said.

MacKenzie continued to probe. 'Everything you write about the young man is the truth?'

She began to cry. 'It is, sir. I was taken in by him. I was tempted by Satan. I let Satan have me as his own. But I have conquered him. The land is well rid of blasphemers!'

There was a sound from the kitchen. He turned to go but hesitated. 'Kerr will trouble you no more, Jane. I need to think about what you've told me.'

'What will happen to me, sir?' Fear was etched on her face.

'Get some rest. I'll be back tomorrow.'

MacKenzie found Agnes in the kitchen. He told Jane to go back to her room. She scampered past Agnes without meeting her eyes. MacKenzie waited for her to leave before addressing Agnes. 'She denies she killed him. She says she and

Mary prayed for the Lord to intervene. They prayed for the Lord to kill him.'

Agnes wiped her hands on her apron and looked up angrily. 'She lies! I know she killed him. She's a conniving little whore! I've seen her on the High Street speaking with men. She plays the pious sister but she's seen in the company of blasphemers.'

MacKenzie dropped his voice. 'She tells me Thomas is Kerr's child.'

Agnes looked down at her hands and wiped them on her apron again. Her voice dropped to a whisper. 'I'll not deny it, sir. But she led the master on. She led him into her own bed as a whore.'

'He no longer visited your bed, Agnes?' asked MacKenzie, provocatively.

Anger flashed across her eyes. 'He has not wanted me for years, not since I grew old and fat. He liked them young like her', she said with venom.

'The first time he came to your bed, Agnes. Did you ask him to?'

She shook her head vehemently, tears formed in her eyes and her voice faltered. 'He told me I would be out on the street if I refused him. I put up with it. I had to do it.'

'Did you vow to have your revenge on him some day? He raped you. He beat you and Thomas. You grew angrier and angrier until you could take it no more. I've seen Thomas' bruises. You saw Kerr in the kitchen in his nightgown. You lost control. You grabbed a knife. You are strong enough to kill him, Agnes.'

The furious expression on her face did not change. 'I did not, sir. I did not kill him. My boy will tell you I never left my bed all night.'

'Are you sure it wasn't your mistress or Mary who killed him?'

'Jane is guilty, sir. She says it herself in the book. She battles with Satan. She is taken by him at night to his coven. She has defiled herself with lust. Thomas read it to me – what he could. She's a wicked creature.' She added defiantly, 'She should burn on the Castle Hill as a witch.'

'Too many poor creatures have met such a fate', said MacKenzie solemnly as he turned and left the kitchen. He found Mrs Kerr sitting in the living chamber with a Bible on her lap, staring out the window. Mary sat across from her with her needlework.

'Will you have some wine, Mr MacKenzie?' she asked.

'No, madam. I must talk to you both again', he said grimly. 'I have disturbing intelligence about your husband.' He decided not to sit but stood between them in the centre of the room. 'Agnes has found a commonplace book kept by Jane.' At the mention of it, Mary looked up and Mrs Kerr turned to face him. 'It describes the events of recent months: her reflections and thoughts and...' He noticed Mary look fearfully at him. 'I've read the whole thing', he continued. 'It paints a black picture of this house, madam. A very black picture. It paints a very black picture of your husband. According to Jane, your husband was a... monster, madam. He was a demon. The pages state both Jane and Mary were abused by him. Agnes has told me she was abused when she entered service also.'

Mrs Kerr moved the Bible from her lap to the table beside her. 'You cannot believe everything Jane writes, Mr MacKenzie. She's a troubled girl. The notion my husband would abuse his own daughter is... ridiculous. I cannot countenance it', she said defiantly.

'So, what Jane describes of her rape and your daughter's rape is fabrication? It is made up by her? For what reason would she say it, madam?' he asked.

'It is lies, Mr MacKenzie. It is the fantasy of a distressed girl. All the sisters know Jane is... highly strung.

Her imagination is prone to flights of fancy. She sees visions. She sees angels and Devils and Satan... everywhere. She sees him on the street and in the fields. She has told me she has seen him in this house!'

MacKenzie turned to Mary. 'What do you say, my dear? Are the things Jane says about your father all lies?'

Mary did not meet his eyes. She put her needlework down and played with a lock of blonde hair which had dropped beneath her bonnet. 'My father would never do such a thing. He was a good man', she said with no hint of emotion.

MacKenzie felt a wave of anger rise within him and cursed them both under his breath in Gaelic. 'You must tell me the truth, Mary. I've been told too many lies in Van Diemen's Land. You deny he mistreated you?'

She nodded her head.

'What of the cuts on your arm?' he asked.

She looked up at him. 'I have passed through temptation', she continued, speaking almost in a trance. 'With prayer I have found the path of righteousness. I am happy in the Lord... now', she added.

'You are close to Jane, are you not, Mary?' asked MacKenzie.

She nodded. 'Jane is not always aware of what is real', she said. 'What belongs to this world and what does not – what belongs to the world of her imaginings. She has fantasies, she has powerful visions. One moment she is speaking to you, the next she is somewhere else.'

'In her book she says that when you told her about your abuse, the pair of you decided to do something about it', said MacKenzie.

She shook her head. 'It's not true, sir.'

'She says she met a young man, the one who is accused of blasphemy and held in the Tolbooth; the one who will hang for it.'

Mary shook her head. 'I know nothing of him. I've never heard her talk about him. She would have told me about him. She loses her sense of this world. She has fought hard with Satan. It has taken its toll on her.'

MacKenzie turned back to Mrs Kerr. 'The father of the blasphemer, Simon Fraser, came to see your husband here. Do you know him or his son?'

'I've never met either of them. It must've been connected to Jacob's business.'

He continued to stare at her. 'There's another thing, madam. Agnes told me Thomas is your husband's child.' He kept his gaze on her, watching her face intently. He noticed a slight twitching of the muscles on her cheek, as if a pulse of truth was trying to find its way out. She finally spoke. 'It's true, Mr MacKenzie. Jacob never lied to me about it. He was tempted by Satan. It was many years ago when he was vulnerable to the Devil. He has atoned for his sins. He has fought hard against Satan. And he was assured of salvation before he died. I should say he is now with the Lord', she said, almost smiling, before adding, 'We brought up the bairn here.'

'That must have been difficult for you', said MacKenzie.

'Life is a trial for us all. It's not easy to enter the gates of Heaven. I have suffered but I have consolation in the sweet words of the Book and the prayers I share with my sisters. I saw Satan leave my husband, gradually, after a long, hard struggle over the years. He was delivered from the sin of lust which he suffered long under. He achieved it through relentless prayer.'

MacKenzie eyed them both suspiciously. Mary took up her needlework and Mrs Kerr opened her Bible. He was feeling frustrated and at something of a loss. He excused himself and left the house, cursing again in a stream of Gaelic as a heavy shower of rain began to fall just as he closed the front door of Van Diemen's Land. By the time he got back to Libberton's Wynd, he was soaked to the skin and his boots were covered in stinking mud. He went to his study and poured himself a whisky, calling Archie to light the fire and serve victuals. After eating, he sat sipping the water of life, gazing into the flames, as it darkened outside. He noticed his right hand was shaking. The events in Van Diemen's Land were having a deeper effect on him than he had expected.

Scougall arrived at ten o'clock. He looked nervous and disturbed. MacKenzie filled a glass from the earthenware pot on the floor and handed the whisky to him. Scougall sipped it without thinking, waiting for the foul taste to register on his tongue.

'What do you think?' asked MacKenzie, after Scougall had taken a chair beside him.

Scougall sighed deeply. 'I fear the influence of the Devil, sir. I fear Jane is a… witch.'

MacKenzie shook his head. 'You're mistaken, Davie.'

'She described visiting a coven and flying to the woods as a bird', Scougall said gravely.

'They were just dreams, Davie. Fearful dreams. Nightmares. The dreams of a disturbed girl. What do you think of her accusations against Kerr?'

'I do not know, sir. If they are true, Kerr was a fiend.'

'Mary and Mrs Kerr deny their truth. They claim Jane has made it all up', said MacKenzie.

Scougall sipped his whisky again and nodded. 'It's possible, sir. But why would she make it all up? I don't understand any of it.'

MacKenzie took out his pipe and filled it with tobacco. Rising from his chair, he stood in front of the fire, staring deep into the flames.

'I've a confession to make, sir', said Scougall uneasily.

MacKenzie turned to face him. 'What confession, Davie?'

'I let Chrissie read it. She saw me reading it. She was worried by the look of horror on my face. I sought her thoughts on it.'

'I told you to show it to no one. She might tell her friends.' There was a flash of anger on MacKenzie's face.

Scougall shook his head vigorously. 'She would never do that, sir. I told her to tell no one. I emphasised lives were at stake. She swore she would not tell a soul.'

MacKenzie looked aggrieved and took a large mouthful of whisky. 'What did she make of it, Davie?'

'She advised caution, sir.'

'Caution, Davie. What do you mean?'

'She said she believed Jane suffered an illness of the mind, rather than demonic possession. The girl was passing through a crisis of some kind. Chrissie thought the book had the ring of truth about it', said Scougall defensively.

MacKenzie smiled and nodded. 'Your wife has more wisdom than you, Davie Scougall.'

Scougall waited for a few moments before he asked, 'Do you know who killed him, sir?'

MacKenzie returned to his chair and sat sipping his whisky. 'I want to sleep on it, Davie. There's one other thing I need your help with. The girl Beatrix, the niece of Umpherston – find out if she was in town at the time of the killing.'

Scougall nodded and looked for his hat, relieved he could escape back to Chrissie. 'There's news, sir. I almost forgot. I meant to tell you when I came in. Alexander Fraser will hang tomorrow. His reprieve has been rejected. He leaves the Tolbooth for the Gallowlee at eleven o'clock.'

MacKenzie looked shocked. 'My God, Davie. Then I'll need you tomorrow morning. I'll write a letter to Mrs Hair, excusing you. The whole city will be out on the street anyway.'

CHAPTER 12

The Execution of a Blasphemer

MACKENZIE HAD A FITFUL night's sleep. He had drunk too much whisky and he drifted in and out of harrowing dreams full of images from Jane's book. Just before he woke, he dreamed he was back at the Hawthorns. After a washing, Meg had put the bed sheets and other clothing out to dry on the lines in the morning sun. He was trying to walk through the sheets and clothes hanging on the ropes in the green beside the river. He was following Jane through them but kept losing sight of her. She would reappear for a moment, before disappearing again; then other characters appeared, one by one – Mary, Mrs Kerr and Agnes – all enticing him onwards, through the endless bed sheets, shirts and shifts until he spotted Jane again. She turned and beckoned him to follow her. After passing through countless more sheets, he came to the edge of the green and found himself on the riverbank.

A figure was standing at the other side, waving to him from across the water. It took a moment for him to see it was not Jane, but a man. He realised joyfully it was his old friend Archibald Stirling, looking rejuvenated, as he was before the cares of the world took their toll on him. Stirling's open, smiling face indicated he was delighted to see MacKenzie. 'You've come to see me at last, John', he said in a calm voice, easily audible over the gurgling water. 'I've been waiting for you. The Van Diemen's Land case is a simple one. But first let me tell you about the Marquis of Montrose...' Stirling smiled and was on the cusp of continuing when MacKenzie woke up.

MacKenzie was annoyed at first, wanting desperately to be back in the dream and talk with his old friend. But there was no way back into the dream. He opened his eyes and saw it was dawn. He had a strange thought which made him smile. Perhaps his old friend had come back from beyond the grave to help him, as he had many times in life. He chuckled as he got out of bed.

At ten minutes to eleven MacKenzie and Scougall were standing outside the Tron Kirk. 'I've learned something important, sir', said Scougall as they turned towards the Tolbooth. 'It's about Beatrix Umpherston.'

'What is it, Davie? Spit it out man!' said MacKenzie impatiently. He was suffering from a slight hangover.

'Beatrix left with Umpherston to stay with relatives in the west a few weeks ago. She only returned with her uncle the day before the sermon at Cramond.'

MacKenzie nodded. 'Then she was not involved in the killing, Davie. Now, follow me.'

They had to struggle through the huge crowds on the High Street. People had come from far and wide to see the execution. It was almost eleven o'clock by the time MacKenzie and Scougall reached the Tolbooth, just in time to see the low door creak open, hushing the crowd to silence. There was a long wait until a figure appeared from the darkness of the interior. Alexander Fraser, dressed in filthy sackcloth, squinted in the brightness, startled by the size of the crowd, a vast shoal of humanity, which began to rain hatred down on him. There was a terrified expression on his lean, gaunt face. Nausea overwhelmed him and he retched onto the cobbles.

Two lines of soldiers indicated the route he had to take through the throng. MacKenzie and Scougall were about five yards away from him, behind the soldiers. MacKenzie called out as Fraser came close, but he was not heard above the braying of the crowd. Fraser moved forwards painfully, proclamations of hatred cast like stones on him. He reached out to touch the ancient wall of the Tolbooth. His hand rested on the stone for a few moments before he staggered off, claiming it as something certain, something moral, something good in the whirlwind of hatred.

A town official ushered him onwards between the soldiers, along the predetermined path, his last moments as public ritual. He walked slowly, heavily on the black cobbles, hard under his bare feet. He was a penitent, sinner, blasphemer before the people.

Time was stilled to heart beats. Fraser counted each one. He would soon be nothing. He almost laughed. He took a few tentative steps into the curses and bitter cries, joyous in his suffering. A raging thirst took hold of him but there was no water to drink. His bowels convulsed but there was nothing left inside him to stain the sackcloth. He staggered onwards, step after painful step, as if walking on shards of glass through stinking puddles of muck. A few incensed onlookers tried to break through the line of soldiers to attack him. Others railed against him as he was said to have railed against God. They were blasphemers unto him. They despised him with every ounce of their being. He was worse than witch or warlock. He was the agent of Satan, the spawn of Antichrist. He threatened their souls and the souls of their children and their children's children until the end of time.

The soldiers' muskets were raised in case he tried to escape or a disturbance broke out. Jacobites were rumoured to be planning an attempt to free him. Fraser wondered if he should run. To be shot would be a blessed release. But he could not run: his legs felt like lead, as if he was wading along the ocean bed, deep under water. Inhaling was like pushing against iron, slowing him to a breathless stagger. The soldiers would drag him back anyway and take him to the gibbet in a cart. The people demanded ritual. He must die before the nation. He was a scapegoat to assuage for their sins.

Fraser stopped at the Mercat Cross, allowing MacKenzie and Scougall to catch up. He stood swaying in the breeze, shivering in the cold. There was nothing more he could suffer. Nothing could increase his pain. He read falteringly from a document in his skeletal hand. His words were faint at first, before gaining in vigour. He had spent hours drafting them. He wanted to say something, an explanation of what had happened to him. But what came out of his mouth was incomprehensible to the surrounding crowd. His tongue felt too large for his mouth. His throat was dry and burning. But he kept on going, oblivious, not realising the words made no sense to anyone. He looked like a madman jabbering.

After a considerable struggle, MacKenzie reached him, Scougall a few paces behind. MacKenzie called out again. 'I've a question, Mr Fraser. Lives are at stake!' But Fraser did not hear. The crowd was almost smothering him. At one point, Scougall was thrust forward and found himself within touching distance of Fraser's dirty sackcloth.

Fraser waited for a response to his reading, some reaction, even from the minister at his arm. A few nods or claps from the crowd, perhaps. But there was nothing. The people cared nothing for his explanation. He was a scapegoat to be sacrificed. He must die for their sins. He looked at the minister but his face was blank.

MacKenzie desperately called out again but his words were lost on the wind that was picking up, a northerly beating the city like a broom. There was murmuring in the crowd, a growing unease. They were impatient with the performance. It had gone on too long already. The weather had turned colder. A covering of clouds was smothering the light of the sun. This was no longer good sport. It had become a bore. They had business to attend to. It was taking up too much of their time. They wanted entertainment, not a sermon from a blasphemer. They did not want explanation or justification. They wanted a spectacle. They thought to themselves: thank God it is not me. A few would decide: I will hold my tongue in the tavern after drinking a bucket of ale, I will be careful when I curse and rail in the ale house, I will go to church on the Sabbath, I will not visit a whore. I will not decry the minister with my cronies.

MacKenzie's attempts to reach him were becoming more desperate as Fraser staggered on like a drunk, oblivious. The minister handed him a tome which he clutched against his chest. It was the book he was said to have blasphemed against, the Bible containing the words of God.

Fraser stopped outside the Tron Kirk, where he had ranted on the steps after a drunken night with his friends. He recalled his mood of exaltation that night, how happy he had been, looking to the future. He would take on the world, sail round the globe and make something of himself. They had all turned against him. Now he wore filthy sackcloth. He looked down at his shivering limbs and bleeding feet. The soldiers thrust him onwards into Leith Wynd where the crowd was still tightly packed all the way back to the tenements. MacKenzie tried to get through again but was thwarted. Scougall struggled to keep up as they were swept past the Correction House and Trinity Kirk and out of the city. Fraser plodded on, head down, into the fields.

At the Gallowlee between Edinburgh and Leith, a gibbet was raised on the open ground. The crowd thinned out, providing an opportunity. MacKenzie ran forward and reached Fraser. At last he was close enough to take hold of his arm. Fraser turned full of fear and incomprehension. No one dared touch the flesh of a blasphemer. 'I beg you. Please, sir.

Lives depend on it... just one question', pleaded MacKenzie. 'Tell me... Did you ask Jane Montgomery to marry you?'

Fraser looked perplexed. He stared at MacKenzie's face for a few moments, before nodding vacantly. Tears were on his cheeks. 'Aye, it's true, sir. I asked the lass. I asked her to marry me. Then she deserted me. She is no better than my classmates who testified against me.'

'Did your father kill Jacob Kerr?' asked MacKenzie.

'Why would he kill him, sir? Kerr was the only one to speak up for me in the Session.'

'Why? Why?' shouted MacKenzie.

'He was bought for five gold guineas.'

Before MacKenzie could say anything else, a soldier thrust him back. He recalled the gold coins lying at the bottom of the kist in Kerr's office, under the array of bonds and notes. Fraser was shoved up the incline towards the gibbet. MacKenzie hung back with Scougall beside him. Another prayer was offered by the minister. The crowd was finally hushed, their anger dissipated by the closeness of death. Thousands had wandered down from the city. A throng as far as the eye could see surrounding the gibbet. At the front were privy councillors and lords and earls and viscounts and baronets and judges and lawyers and merchants, and the men of God and godly dames – the unco guid of the nation of Scotland.

A look of bewilderment was on Fraser's face. The hangman offered his hand, helping him onto the scaffold. A hood was placed over his head, slowly, carefully, the noose round his neck. Fraser's last thoughts were of his mother, her love enfolding him as a child in bed with a cat warming his feet, drifting into slumber, just as Christ should embrace his people, he thought; not like this, surely, not like this, never like this... He dropped.

Scougall looked away in horror and MacKenzie closed his eyes, shaking his head in despair. A young life extinguished for nothing. The savagery of the Christian message of sin disgusted him to the core. Fraser's body swung in the breeze; his broken neck at an awful angle. They stood for a while, letting the crowd drift past, heading back towards the city.

MacKenzie turned to Scougall and sighed. 'I'm afraid we must pay a visit to the Kirk, Davie.'

CHAPTER 13

A Killing in Van Diemen's Land

THEY BOTH KEPT their thoughts to themselves as they plodded back to the city. MacKenzie was going over in his head the possible chain of events that resulted in the killing in Van Diemen's Land. Scougall was thinking of Chrissie. St Giles Kirk was dark and silent inside, the door of the minister's study locked. MacKenzie did not hesitate. He took a few steps back, lowered his shoulder and ran into the door like a Highland bull. The lock gave way easily and MacKenzie found himself inside, trying to keep his balance. He went straight to Sharp's desk, Scougall following nervously. The Kirk Session minute book lay open. MacKenzie bent over and began to flick through the pages.

'Here it is, Davie!' MacKenzie put his finger on the page and read slowly. 'The case of Alexander Fraser put to the vote. All voted in favour of the case being sent up to the Justiciary except Mr Jacob Kerr who argued the Session should show leniency this being the accused's first offence.' He looked up at Scougall and shook his head before adding, 'The power of gold, Davie!'

When they reached Cumming's Court, a small crowd was gathered outside the door of Van Diemen's Land. MacKenzie pushed his way to the front, fearful of what he might find. On the ground lay a crumpled body, a pool of blood around a head peppered in patches of blonde hair. Another woman was leaning over the body, crying distraughtly.

A voice from the crowd spoke in horror, 'She jumped from up there!' The woman pointed to the top floor of Van Diemen's Land. The garret window was open.

The woman on the ground crying forlornly was Mrs Kerr. 'My beautiful child! My beautiful child taken as well!' she began to wail.

MacKenzie looked down on the thin features of Mary Kerr. He had expected to see the face of Jane Montgomery. 'My God', he said aloud. 'What Hell hath religion made in this land!'

An hour later MacKenzie and Scougall were sitting in the living chamber of Van Diemen's Land, Mrs Kerr and Jane opposite them on the couch, Agnes on the chair beside them. Mary's body had been taken to the morgue and Thomas sent away to play. MacKenzie spoke solemnly to them all. 'I've asked Mr Scougall to record everything that is said. I urge you to tell the truth and nothing else.'

Rising to his feet, MacKenzie recalled the first time he had pleaded before the Court of Session as a young advocate back in the early 1660s. He recalled how nervous he was. It was always better to make a case on your feet, he had been told then. He began to pace slowly about the room, the only sound the creaking floorboards under his boots and the scraping of Scougall's quill on the paper of his notebook.

MacKenzie first addressed Mrs Kerr in a calm voice. 'Your family moved into Van Diemen's Land a dozen years ago and employed Agnes as a servant. Perhaps those early years were happy ones, I do not know. But your husband began to show interest in Agnes and forced himself on her. Sadly, it's a common enough story.'

Agnes blurted out: 'I did not seek his advances, sir. When I was pregnant, he left me alone. Then it started again, not long after I gave birth. He came to my room even when the bairn was there. I hated him!'

MacKenzie raised his hand to indicate he would hear her in good time. He turned back to Mrs Kerr. 'You accepted the child in your house, madam. However, things changed as Mary grew older. Your husband's perversity reached an even higher pitch. He began to abuse his own daughter, adding the monstrous crime of incest to that of rape. He made a fine elder of the Kirk, beating his wife when she protested. You bore long years of suffering, madam. I can barely imagine how much you suffered. I'm not surprised you sought solace in the sisterhood. And finally Jane came into the household. I do not know why you sought her out. She was probably desired by your husband. Did you hope perhaps that she might deflect attention from your daughter? If that was the case madam, you are culpable in your husband's crimes. For Jane was raped too. Jacob Kerr was a devil who used his position as pious elder to cover his fiendish nature. I know you are all glad he's dead. It was a household more akin to Hell than any I have come upon. It was soaked in hypocrisy and countless crimes have been committed behind its walls over the years.'

Mrs Kerr cried out: 'What was I to do, sir? What could I do? I prayed to God for deliverance from him. I prayed for it every day of my life. I begged God. I got down on my knees every night and begged Him. But year after year it continued. It would stop for a couple of months and I thought we were free. But then it started again. Now I've lost everything. He has taken every last thing from me. Satan has taken every last drop! I did not ask for Jane to be brought here as you say. It was his doing! He demanded it! And I could not refuse him. I could never refuse him.'

Jane turned to her and spoke softly. 'Mary is with the angels, mistress. There's no doubt she is taken by the Lord. She will live with Him for evermore. She was good and meek. She was promised everlasting glory. We shall both see her again, when we leave this world. I'm sure of it. We will see her again. We will laugh together as we have done in the fields with our sisters. We will see her again.'

MacKenzie waited for Mrs Kerr to gather herself before continuing. 'I now turn to the crime at hand, the one I was asked to investigate, not the others committed in this house which have been manifold and which went unpunished, but the killing of Jacob Kerr.' MacKenzie continued to address Mrs Kerr. 'Your motive for killing your husband is clear, madam. You were an abused wife of over 20 years, your beloved daughter was debauched and driven to cutting herself. Your only relief was hope for something better in the next life.'

He turned to Agnes. 'You were molested by your master and you and your son beaten relentlessly by him.'

And then he addressed Jane. 'You also had a motive, Jane. You were abused almost as soon as you entered this house.' MacKenzie stopped for a moment before adding, 'Thomas had a motive but I thought it doubtful he could be the killer. Finally, there was Mary. She looked too weak to kill on her own but if aided by another it was possible.'

He stood for a few moments beside the portrait of Kerr and his wife and observed it carefully before turning and continuing. 'At first it seemed the crime was carried out after a disturbed robbery. But there was evidence which pointed to another interpretation: first, the clumsy breaking of the lock of the back door from the inside, as indicated by debris on the floor of the kitchen and marks around the lock and secondly the discovery of a knife in Mrs Kerr's chamber. How could a thief hide it there?

'I was convinced that someone in the house was involved. The discovery of a fragment of cloth in the range of the kitchen, suggested an item of clothing had been hastily destroyed on the night of the killing. The piece of cotton, more expensive than linen, intimated it did not belong to one of the servants. This implicated Mrs Kerr or Mary. And finally, the atmosphere in the house which I felt from the start: pain and anguish and fear, as soon as I walked across the threshold. I soon surmised it was not for the loss of Mr Kerr. I therefore deduced that someone within the household was involved in the killing, either in carrying it out or being aided by an outsider. I have been able to determine that a number of possible candidates from outside the house, Beatrix Umpherston, Simon Fraser and Alexander Fraser, were not involved. As I learned more about life in the house, it was evident you all had a motive for killing him. He had raped or beaten you all over the years. I'm sure you all despised him but power is a strange thing. I doubt not that you all dreamed of the day he was dead. I'm sure you all fantasied about killing him but as far as raising a weapon and turning it on him – that was something else. It was too risky. What if you failed? What would he do to you then? Would he turn the weapon on you without hesitation?'

MacKenzie paused for a few moments, taking out his pipe and stuffing it with tobacco. He stood in the silent room like a smoking statue, puffing away. 'There was another vital clue that came to me this morning with a little help from an old friend.' He smiled to himself, recalling Stirling's knowing expression across the river in the dream. 'When I examined the house the morning after the murder, I found used nightgowns belonging to Agnes and Thomas under their pillows. There was no sign of blood on either of them, which there would have been if they had stabbed Kerr during the night, unless they were naked when they killed him, which I thought unlikely. However, there were only laundered nightgowns in the rooms of Mary, Jane and Mrs Kerr and no sign of any soiled ones in their rooms or the laundry. Where had the nightgowns they had worn on the night of the killing gone? It seemed likely to me that they had been destroyed.

This placed Mrs Kerr, Mary and Jane in the kitchen during or at some point soon after the killing.

'The wounds on the corpse indicated the weapon was driven down into Kerr's back from above. Kerr must have been leaning over or on his knees when attacked. Given his bulk, it was likely he was surprised, so he could not easily defend himself. I surmised it was likely more than one person was involved in his killing. There was also the blonde hair under the table which suggested Mary had hidden there. Finally, there was Jane's book found by Agnes. A statement in it hinted that Agnes could have been the killer but I discounted this. If she had been, would she have risked telling me about the book? On the other hand, a number of sections suggested Jane and Mary were planning to kill him, although this was not conclusive and was denied by Jane, who claimed they sought prayer only as their weapon. There was also the veracity of the diary itself. Was it just the fantasy of a disturbed girl? I believe I've been able to establish the book is truthful.' MacKenzie stopped briefly to emphasise what followed.

He moved forward to stand a couple of yards in front of Mrs Kerr, Agnes and Jane. They all had their heads bowed, not meeting his gaze. 'Let me tell you what I think happened in Van Diemen's Land, ladies. The key event in this dismal tale was the arrival of Jane in the house. Her arrival set off a chain of events which, I believe, led to the killing.

First of all, we know Jacob had an eye on her from the start. He had ordered his wife to obtain her for him. But another relationship developed between Jane and Mary, a close, tender and intense one. They became sisters in Christ and shared everything. Mary eventually told Jane of her abuse at the hands of her father, and Jane told Mary about her own molestation. In sharing their woes, they obtained some recompense. It also gave them a sense of power.

It enabled them to act together to kill him.' MacKenzie had moved opposite Jane who continued to look down at her hands. 'Jane and Mary hatched a plan to be rid of him. I do not know who came up with the details. I will tell you what I think happened.'

MacKenzie moved off towards the window and looked down on the courtyard as he continued to address them. 'Towards midnight on 13 June or in the early hours of 14 June, Jane went down to the kitchen. She had approached Kerr earlier in the day, perhaps saying she had a matter to discuss with him in private, a matter involving her struggles with sin. It was safest they met as far away as possible from the rest of the household. She knew he could be enticed. Sure enough, he readily agreed. And so that night he was eager to get the household off to bed. Jane came down to the kitchen and waited, perhaps sitting on the chair left facing the corridor. Kerr appeared in his nightgown. As he lent down over her, no doubt cursing how he was tempted by the Devil and other such drivel she grabbed him round the neck. Jane held on to him as tightly as she could and did not let go. Perhaps he thought initially she was showing him some passionate encouragement and he did not fight her off for a few moments. Jane knew she could not let go; she had to hold on for her life and Mary's life depended on it. Mary was hiding under the table with a knife. She came out of the shadows and stabbed her father in the back. The strokes were delivered quickly, one after the other. At this point, he realised what was happening and no doubt began to struggle ferociously. He may have pulled out a handful of his own daughter's hair in the fight which I found later under the table. But Jane held on, as if her eternal soul depended on it. Jane did not let go. Jane would never let go. For she had to give Mary enough time to inflict a mortal wound. Mary unleashed a frenzy of stabs as the built-up hatred of years flooded out of her. Did she finally slice his neck or did she hand the knife to Jane as he lay dying on the floor? I do not know. He was finally dispatched from this world.' MacKenzie turned to Jane and waited for a few silent moments before asking, 'Is that what happened, my dear?'

Jane finally met his gaze. She spoke softly, her eyes glazed by tears. 'I will tell you the truth, sir. I must tell the truth now. I will do it for Mary's sake. What you describe is... close to the truth. But it is not the way it happened, although it was what we planned. You see, the Lord told Mary to do it. She had dreamed of a knife going into him, and that whatever became of us afterwards, we were assured of meeting again in Heaven. She knew her father was possessed by Satan. She knew his soul belonged to Antichrist. We were fighting Satan by doing it, sir. God sanctioned it.'

'And that was not all', interrupted MacKenzie, turning to Mrs Kerr. 'You had heard something during the night and you came down to the kitchen. You were faced by an awful sight. Your husband lying dead on the kitchen floor in a scene of bloody murder. Emotions flooded through you: horror at the gore, fear of what would happen to you all but also unbridled joy that he was gone forever. Would the three of you face the gallows? You had to act quickly. The girls were standing in their bloody garments, unable to move following the act of killing. But you were able to act rationally. It occurred to me there had to be a rational intelligence responding to the aftermath. It could not have been Mary or Jane after the frenzy of the killing. You told them to take off their blood-soaked garments. You threw them into the range and destroyed them in the flames, leaving only a tiny fragment. You went up to the ground floor and broke the lock of the door. You took the keys from your husband's belt and opened both kists. You transferred all the documents in the smaller one into the larger and locked it again, leaving the smaller one open with the keys in the lock. Kerr was a meticulous merchant who would never store his cash and paper in such a random manner. You told the girls to say absolutely nothing, except for Mary to acknowledge she heard something during the night, perhaps a thief breaking in. They were to admit nothing other than that Kerr was a good Christian. If they said anything more, they would all hang. You would make it look like robbery and all would be well. You cleaned their naked bodies with rags which you also burned. Finally, you cleaned the knife. Why did you not return it to its place beside the others? Because you wanted to make it look like it had been taken by the thief. Instead, you wrapped it in cloth and hid it in your chamber, perhaps planning to get rid of it later. Then, exhausted, you all returned to bed, leaving your husband to be found by Agnes in the morning.'

MacKenzie turned to Scougall who was busy scribbling. 'I believe Mary killed her father, aided by Jane. Mary could not live with the guilt of her abuse and the crime of patricide and so she destroyed herself.'

Suddenly, Mrs Kerr rose to her feet with an expression of agony on her face and shrieked. 'And he deserved it, sir! He has killed his own daughter and now we will all hang for it! He has brought the fury of Hell into this sorry household!'

MacKenzie felt a slither of satisfaction at his reconstruction of the killing but the overriding emotion was deep sorrow for the three women.

'You are wrong, sir', Mrs Kerr continued, shaking her head in despair. 'It was not Mary or Jane who killed him. It was me! I killed him!'

MacKenzie raised his eyebrows and Scougall looked up from his notetaking.

Mrs Kerr continued, her voice breaking with emotion. 'I heard a noise in the night as you said. I came down to the kitchen as you described, Mr MacKenzie. I found a scene from my worst nightmare – my daughter cowering under the table with a look of utter terror on her face, tearing out her own hair. My husband, his back to me, pinning Jane to the floor and raising his fist to strike her. I realised in an instant they had tried to kill him but failed. Mary was paralysed by fear. At the vital moment she could not act and was easily thrown aside by him. Jane would face brutal retribution. I did not hesitate. It was as if God directed me. I raised my forefinger to my mouth to tell Mary to remain silent. I picked up a knife from the stand beside the sink. I crept up behind him and as he reigned obscenities down on Jane, I slit his throat. I slit his throat, God forgive me. I slit his throat. Then as the blood gushed from the wound over Jane, I stabbed him in the back, once, twice, a dozen times and more. I could not stop myself. Every day I lived in Van Diemen's Land was torture, every hour, every minute of every day.' She broke down in tears and was comforted by Jane. There was silence for a minute before she continued.

'On our wedding night he confessed his whoring to me. He told me the number of women he had fornicated with. He described all the abominable acts done with them. He told me in tears how he had fought Satan. Satan had tempted him with lust. But he would be tempted no more. I would be the receptacle of his lust and I was for a time. It was a terrible time. I will not ever talk of the perversities he forced me to engage in, night after night. I had no one to turn to. How could I talk of such things with my own mother or friends? But he soon tired of me and turned his attention on Agnes.'

She turned to Agnes and put her hand on hers. 'I'm truly sorry for it, Agnes. God knows I am. I prayed for your deliverance every day. Then, when I thought he could stoop no lower, I found him debauching Mary. I wanted to kill him then. I tried to but he stopped me – beat me to pulp with his belt as he had done countless times before. I almost killed myself but

I could not do it. I had to go on living for Mary. He told me if I killed myself, he would make Mary's life even worse. He would only stop molesting her if another servant was brought into the house, one that was to his liking. So he chose Jane, having seen her with my sisters. He showed me not an ounce of tenderness in 20 years of marriage. I was married to Satan, Mr MacKenzie. I hope he rots in Hell for eternity!'

There was an intense stillness in the room when she finished. Scougall stopped recording the awful details of her confession. The Tron Kirk Bell began to chime in the distance. MacKenzie counted four strokes.

'What will happen to us?' asked Agnes, breaking the silence.

'You are the only innocent one', said Jane. 'You'll be alright.'

'I will lose my place, though. I'll be shunned', she said. 'What about Thomas' future?'

MacKenzie took a seat on the chair beside Scougall. 'You must decide your fate for yourselves', he said, resignedly.

'How do you mean, sir?' asked Mrs Kerr, tearfully.

'It's true that if the case goes to court, you and Jane will hang for it. I have no doubt about it. You were both involved in the killing. The court will ignore your husband's crimes. But there is another way', he said.

'How so, sir?' asked Mrs Kerr.

'I will make my report to the Advocate. A thief broke into Van Diemen's Land on the night of 14 June. He was disturbed by Mr Kerr. The thief killed him and made off with some money, the exact amount uncertain. The thief has disappeared. Many people pass in and out of the city every day. My Lord is a busy man. He will accept my account. It will cause little stir during these momentous days. The killing is already forgotten as the weighty matter of the Kirk dominates everything.' MacKenzie turned to Jane. 'You have an offer of a place in the north of England. You should take it. Leave this realm for good, change your name and make a new life there. Never return to Scotland.' She nodded expressionlessly.

He then spoke to Agnes. 'You must say nothing of what has happened in this house. You must put aside your hatred of Jane for the sake of your son and Mrs Kerr. If you tell anyone anything, you will all hang. I believe Mrs Kerr will support you and your son, either in this house or in another place.'

Finally, he turned to Mrs Kerr. 'You will be haunted to the end of your days by the loss of your daughter. I can offer you no comfort and you will suffer until the day you die. But looking after Thomas may provide a little recompense. Make him a good man and maybe something can come out of this miserable affair.'

MacKenzie took the slim volume from his pocket and returned it to Jane. 'I would burn this if I were you.' She looked down at it for a moment, then went to the fire and dropped it into the flames.

'Place all your notes there also, Davie', ordered MacKenzie. Scougall looked baffled. 'If Kerr was not killed', added MacKenzie, 'he would have abused these women until the end of their days.' Scougall rose and went to the fire. Without hesitation, he dropped his notebook into it. He thought of Chrissie and smiled to himself. She would be pleased by what they were doing.

A disturbing thought passed through Scougall's mind as he watched the paper catch light and shrink to nothing. Why would God create such a creature as Jacob Kerr? Why would He make a being that wreaked havoc in the world, one that did not do an iota of good? But he had no answer, other than that Satan was involved, somehow.

The Hawthorns

10 July 1690

MacKenzie and Scougall were sitting together on a wooden bench beside the fountain in the small courtyard outside the library at the Hawthorns. Scougall was enjoying the warm sun on his face and the soporific sound of gurgling water. 'You have your presbytery at last, Davie', MacKenzie as he put down the news sheet he had been reading, but he could not help adding, 'I doubt much good will come of it.'

Scougall spoke tentatively. He was relaxed and not in the mood to argue. 'A nation at peace – perhaps with itself – at last... I hope so, sir.'

'Hardly, Davie. Ireland is in turmoil. The armies will clash in that country soon. In the Highlands, some chiefs will not swear allegiance to William. Soldiers gather across Europe for a bigger struggle.'

'It might take some time, sir. I know you dislike presbytery. I cannot blame you. You've lost much: your position in the Session, your honour. But most people will be happy with the new settlement.'

MacKenzie was on the point of saying more, when their attention was suddenly taken by the appearance of a young child of about a year old, wobbling unsteadily on his feet at the French doors of the library. The child's face broke into a wild laugh and he staggered towards them, recognising his grandfather. MacKenzie rose and scooped him up in his arms, the boy squealing in delight as he was tossed in the air and caught. MacKenzie whispered Gaelic endearments in his ear.

'This is Mr Davie Scougall, Geordie', he said, reverting to English. 'He's an old friend of your grandfather. Although we disagree about politics, it does not matter much', he smiled. 'We will not take up swords to settle our differences.' MacKenzie cuddled the bairn and winked at Scougall. 'I hope for one thing, Davie. I hope Scotland is a more tolerant country when Geordie is a man. If that's the case, all this strife will have been worth it.'

Scougall held his hand out for the bairn, quite taken with him. 'I believe it will be so, sir. Things will settle down, as they always do. Folk will turn their attention to other things than politics. Scotland may prosper with a little luck, eventually.'

Scougall held Geordie's tiny hand, captivated by him. He had not told anyone the news yet. They were waiting a few more weeks to make sure. Chrissie was with child. He could not quite believe it. He would be a father himself within the year. He prayed under his breath all would go well.

They heard footsteps approaching and Elizabeth appeared from the door with a worried expression. She was searching for the child. Her face immediately lightened when she saw he was safe. 'There you are, you wee rascal!' She took him from MacKenzie, tickling him under the ribs. Geordie let out another squeal of delight and they all laughed. She turned to Scougall. 'It's good to see you again, Davie.'

'I'm glad to see you, Elizabeth', he replied, seriously.

'Davie Scougall, a married man. I can hardly believe it', she mocked him. 'How do you find your bedfellow?'

Scougall was annoyed by her forwardness but when he thought of Chrissie, he was struck by something. He had long loved Elizabeth from afar but he felt differently about her now. He still admired her beauty and poise and elegance. She was a bit older than the last time he had seen her but she was still a beauty. However, his infatuation was over. The thought sent a spasm of delight through him and firmed his confidence. 'I find her very well indeed, Elizabeth.' His face beamed, but not from embarrassment – rather, with pride. 'I must return to her now. We'll both visit you sometime soon. Chrissie would love to see the gardens.'

'Will you not stay for dinner, Davie?' she asked.

'No, I must be off. I'm a married man, indeed', he smiled at her and then turned to MacKenzie. 'Perhaps a game of golf next week, sir. And before I forget, I meant to tell you. There is news from Van Diemen's Land. Jane has left for a position in the north of England. The rest of the household are settled in a new apartment in Mylne's Court. Van Diemen's Land is up for sale. I will keep an eye on Thomas. If he progresses well, I'll find an apprenticeship for him.'

MacKenzie patted Scougall on the shoulder. 'I'm glad of it, Davie. What about Mrs Kerr?'

'I've heard she's much taken up with the sisterhood', Scougall replied.

MacKenzie shook his head. It was a waste of a good-looking woman. He remembered his feelings for her in the living chamber of Van Diemen's Land. She would never be separated from her God. It was a shame. He smiled to himself. Perhaps it was time he found a wife himself. But the thought sent a melancholic twinge through his heart.

'I'm off on business for Mrs Hair tomorrow. I must attend her trading interests in the west', said Scougall enthusiastically, taking his hat to leave.

'Where are you bound, Davie? Barbados or Jamaica?' MacKenzie asked with a glint of irony in his eye.

Scougall shook his head. 'I'm not travelling as far as that, sir. I must go to the town of Glasgow. I've never been so far west in my life.'

Acknowledgements

I WOULD LIKE TO thank my wife Julie as always for all her love and support. Thanks to my children Jamie, Robbie and Katie, and to their partners Izzy, Laura and Conor for their love and good company. Special thanks to Carrie Hutchison and Maia Gentle for editing the text and designing the cover, and to Gavin MacDougall for keeping faith with the MacKenzie series.

I have found Michael F. Graham's, *The Blasphemies of Thomas Aikenhead* (Edinburgh, 2013) and *Memoirs, or Spiritual Exercises of Elisabeth West* (Edinburgh, 1807), particularly useful historical sources for the spiritual crisis in late 17th century Scotland.